SUMMER UNPLUGGED

BOOK ONE

AMY SPARLING

❀ Created with Vellum

CHAPTER 1

I kissed a boy on the cheek and it got me grounded for the whole summer. A measly, meaningless cheek kiss. Mom freaked. Ian bolted without saying bye. Mom yelled for an eternity and then stormed back inside leaving me fully clothed, bra unhooked, feet dangling in the pool. It sucks that she came home from work an hour earlier than usual, but at least she wasn't two hours earlier when Ian and me were in the pool, doing way more than cheek-kissing. I know he's the one for me. But she doesn't see it that way.

She freaks about the stupidest things sometimes. But she always says I've lost her trust so, my bad. It wasn't the kiss that pissed her off. It's probably the fact that she banned Ian from our house two months ago when he was thrown into juvi for selling weed. I never smoked it with him so it's not really a big deal. And then last week she banned me from seeing him when she caught us skipping school together. In my bed. Anyhow the details don't matter anymore because she finally had enough of my being a normal teenager and she's decided to take away my life. I mean my cell phone. Same thing.

At least it's Friday. My flat iron hisses as I rake it through my hair until I hear mom's bedroom TV turn off around 10:30 as it always does. I finish my hair, throw on some makeup with extra sparkly eyeliner and call Becca. She isn't my first friend of choice but, she has a car and is a total pushover.

"I need a ride to the senior's party," I say. "And I'm thinking you could totally use a passenger."

"Bayleigh," she groans. It's obvious she's annoyed with me, but she'll get over it because without me, she wouldn't be invited to a party this big. "Your house is twenty minutes out of the way, if I take you home too I'll have to leave forty minutes before my curfew."

"Just get me. Please?" My knuckles are white on the clear plastic corded phone. I haven't used this thing in forever. No one uses house phones anymore. Silence on the other end. "I'm sorry," I say with sincerity. "Just please come get me. I'll find another ride home."

"Fine," she says, ending the call.

An unearthly wave of heat rests over the town as I wait on the front porch for her to arrive. The humidity will ruin my hair if she makes me wait another five minutes. Two minutes later she pulls into the driveway, headlights on. What. An. Idiot.

I run to her car and swing open the passenger door. "Turn off the lights," I hiss. She fumbles on the dashboard, feeling for the switch. She's only been driving two months and she's not nearly as skilled as I am in the art of being stealthy and sneaking out. Becca's just not the kind of person who sneaks out. She's not like me. I should forgive her slipups and not scream since she did go out of her way to give me a ride.

But then the front door swings open with a violent swoosh and now I know I won't ever forgive her. Because I've just been caught.

CHAPTER 2

Ninety days of no cell phone. Ninety days of no Ian. Ninety days of grounded.

I am not going to stand for this. I live one block away from the high school. It's Monday morning, the second to last day of school before summer break. Ian hasn't heard from me all day and he's probably going crazy, thinking I'm lying dead in a ditch somewhere.

No one does work in History class because we took finals two days ago and there's nothing left to do. I ask to go to the nurse. Mr. Garcia shoos me out of the door the second I say the word cramps and then I walk home instead of to the nurse's office.

Mom's dresser drawers come up empty. So does

her nightstand, closet and under her bed. Under her mattress. Behind all her jars of anti-wrinkle cream and under the stack of bills she hasn't paid yet. I can't think of any other places to look for my cell phone. I try calling it but it goes straight to voicemail which makes sense because my battery has a sucky lifespan.

Defeated, I go to my room hoping that bag of peanut M&Ms is still on my nightstand. My phone is on the middle of my bed, a note on top of it.

Please be good. Love, Mom

Oh hell yes. Mom will get an amazing Mother's Day gift this year. I try calling Ian but he doesn't answer which is odd because he goes to work at the movie theater at three, so he should be awake by now. I try leaving him a cute, sexy voicemail but it probably comes out kind of lame. Oh well, that's how I am and he likes it.

I walk back to school because ditching the rest of the day would surely get my phone taken away again. I sleep through the next three classes until sixth period. Sign language. My five-year-old cousin Sarra is deaf. Besides her parents, I am the only one who can talk to her because I've put forth an effort to learn the language. Plus my teacher is hands down, the best teacher in this entire school.

Becca and Matt perform a sign language version

of the Metallica song Ride the Lightning. Even in sign language it's obvious that Becca is in love with Matt. I feel bad for making out with him freshman year. She says she didn't like him back then, but the wistful look on her face when she sees him tells me that her crush didn't develop overnight.

My phone vibrates. It's a text from Ian – finally.

Babe its hard hanging out with you when your mom's a psycho.

WTF? I write back, phone hidden in the sleeve of my hoody. Ian and I have a flip-flop relationship. It's not even a real relationship since he refuses to call me his girlfriend. Sometimes he claims to love me more than life itself. Other times he flips and wants nothing to do with me. I guess this is another flip. I'm sad but, not really. He'll come back to me.

You coming to my party tomorrow?

I stare at the screen, forced to think about what I haven't wanted to think about. Ian's huge end-of-school bash. Just about everyone is invited and it is vital that I be there. But Mom didn't let me go to a much smaller party last weekend and she wasn't too thrilled when she caught me sneaking out. I write back *Yes,* despite knowing there's a better chance of me being valedictorian than going to that party.

Tuesday night I go to bed defeated, Mom having turned down every bit of begging I did. Bargaining, groveling, crying, guilt-tripping. Nothing worked.

CHAPTER 3

Ian didn't reply to any of my texts last night. And so far, he hasn't replied to any of my morning texts either. If we were officially dating, I'd threaten to break up with him.

My phone is set on super loud and vibrate mode but I check it again, just in case. Nothing. I shove it back on the nightstand, grinding my teeth. Then I wriggle back under the covers. It's a beautiful Saturday morning, the first day of summer break and I have nothing to do but lay in bed all day because I am grounded. And they say we have it better than our grandparents did. Right. I groan, pull the pillow over my head, think seriously about suffocating myself but I know that would never work.

I wish there was some kind of over-the counter-coma pill. A pretty blue pill that would knock me into a three-month coma, ending on the first day of my sophomore year. School sucks, but at least I'd get to see Ian because he promised me he would come back to school for his senior year.

Mom calls for my little brother and me to come to breakfast. Bentley's socked feet run and slide down the hallway. Hardwood floors are fun like that. Run, slide, run, slide. Ugh. Ten-year-olds have life way better than I do.

I crawl out of bed, grab my phone and trudge to the kitchen. My hands feel sweaty. The morning after fighting with Mom is always awkward. Chances are, she won't mention it anyway. She always yells at me and then on the next day she pretends that nothing happened. Maybe that is some kind of psychological parenting ploy. Or maybe it's all she knows how to do – mothers are the nurturing type. I don't have a father to inflict punishments, so nothing happens when I get in trouble. I smile. I love being the bastard child of a single mom. No punishments – just yelling.

And then she starts yelling at me from the kitchen and I change my mind.

"Bayleigh!" Her voice carries down the hallway. I

cringe, but at least she didn't use the middle name too.

"Yeah? I mean, Ma'am?" I say. Bentley's sitting at the bar playing his Nintendo 3DS with the volume way too loud.

"You left the TV and the hall light on all night." Mom rips into me almost like it was rehearsed. "Unless you want to start paying the light bill, you better turn everything off, dammit."

"Okay," I say. She flips a pancake with unnecessary spatula force. "And you haven't fed Patch all week and you know that's your job."

I sigh. "Yes ma'am."

She sets a plate of food in front of Bentley and he digs in, somehow still managing to play his video game. She's not going to make a plate for me so I get up and get my own. Between layering pancakes and syrup, my phone vibrates from the counter. I leap around Mom, slamming into her shoulder as I lurch for my phone. It's a text from Ian.

"Jesus, Bayleigh." Mom's coffee splashes out of her cup. "You almost knocked me over trying to read a text message? Seriously?" Mom is moody today. I open the message.

"It's important," I say, looking at my phone.

Hey

My heart warms. It's only one word, but it's a word from Ian. I type a reply, read over it, decide it sucks and type a new message. I press send. When I come back to reality, Mom is still gripping her coffee. Her lips are pursed into a frown. She's been watching me.

"What?" I ask.

She reaches out to me with the hand that isn't dripping with coffee. "Give me your phone."

"What? No." I pull the handset to my chest, press the lock key just in case she forces it out of my grasp. She can't read my messages without the password.

"You're grounded. That means no parties, no boys, and now it means no cell phone. I tried to give it back to you, but this just won't work." Her hand, palm up waits for me to surrender my phone. It seems hopeless to try now, but I do what I do best. I cry.

"Please, Mom. Please *please* don't take my phone." I grab her, hold her tight. She hugs me back, showing the weakness in her parental armor. "I'll be good, I promise." She sighs. Pulls me back. Her face is more wrinkly this close. My hand vibrates and I want to read Ian's reply so bad, but I know now is not the time.

The last tear rolls down my cheek. The lines in

her forehead soften. "Fine," she says, retracting her hand. I almost start jumping up and down. "Thanks, Mom." I hug her again. She freaks because the bacon is burning and rushes over to it.

"You're still grounded," she says as she rescues the bacon, her back facing me.

"Okay." I smile. It's not like I can't find a way to see Ian when she's at work.

CHAPTER 4

After breakfast, Mom and Bentley go shopping for new baseball gear for his summer league. I retreat to my room and play on Facebook. Ian's profile has been tagged with fifty-six new photos from last night's party. I have been tagged in exactly zero photos. Because I didn't get to go.

My blood boils the moment I click on the first photo. Forty of the photos were added by some girl named Stacia who looks like she could very well be a Victoria's Secret model. She definitely doesn't go to our school. One thing is for sure – I've never seen her before. What the hell kind of name is that anyway? I click on her profile. It's private. Dammit.

I go back to his photos and sink into a depression

hole that gets deeper with every click. Stacia's captions bother me: TWO HOTTIES. It's a self-taken close-up of her and Ian. I scrutinize every detail, every pixel. At least her hand is around him, not the other way around.

The next several photos chronicle their game of beer pong. The last one has Ian looking tipsy yet adorable. I save it to my desktop. He's holding a Styrofoam cup in one hand, two ping pong balls in the other. I LOVE HIS BALLS! XOXO is the caption. That's it. I text Becca.

Who the hell is this Stacia girl?

My phone rings, Becca's smiling face showing up on the screen. "Who is she?" I say instead of hello.

"I dunno, I didn't even know her name till I saw the photos online."

"Was she flirting with him all night?"

"Umm," she thinks for a moment. She's stalling to save my feelings.

"I knew it," I say. "What a bitch."

"She was all over every guy last night, Bayleigh. I don't think you should worry."

I go back to Stacia's page and stare at the Facebook warning telling me I have to be her friend to view her full profile. "Are you online right now?" I ask her.

"You know I am."

"Add her as a friend, and then let me know if Ian's posted any comments on her page." She whines. It takes a few more minutes to coerce her into doing it, and I even have to pull the "You know I would do the same for you" card, but she finally agrees.

Now I have two things on the agenda for today: wait for Ian's next text message and wait for Becca to call me back with details on Stacia's page. I watch an episode of Supernatural, paint my nails, brush my teeth and stare at the ceiling for a million hours until he finally writes me back. His texts are so sporadic, but getting them totally makes my day.

Ian: *I want to see you.*

I write back: *I wish. Mom will be home soon.*

I refresh my homepage. No new comments. My phone vibrates.

Ian: *Send me a pic.*

Me: *That's not the same as seeing me...*

I know it's totally against the rules to double text a guy you're crushing on, but I do it anyway.

Me: *Speaking of photos, I just saw a ton of you and some girl??? on your profile...*

Fifteen minutes later, no reply. Shit, that was a mistake. I bite my lip and do something terrible. I triple text.

Me: *Where'd ya go?*

He replies immediately. *Waiting on your pic.*

Ugh. I send him a photo from my phone's storage of images. It's of me and a kitten. He replies: *sexy... anymore?*

Me: *Who was that girl?*

My thumbs ache from pressing the screen so hard.

Ian: *No one, pic please? I miss you.*

I don't know why he needs so many photos of me when there are hundreds online. I turn my phone's camera on myself, stick out my tongue and cross my eyes and snap a photo. I send it to him.

Ian: *Come on, you can do sexier than that.*

Me: *Sexier? What does that mean? I'm not Sports Illustrated model.*

Ian: *Shirtless.*

My heart races. No. Freaking. Way.

Twenty-five persuasive texts later and I'm standing in the bathroom in my bra, phone camera ready. I so cannot do this. The neighbor's dog starts barking and soon our dog Patch joins him. I know all guys care about sex but why does he want this photo so badly?

I bet Stacia would send him a photo. I wonder if she already has.

I shift my leg, tilt my hips and shoulder like a model. Purse my lips. I look silly. I switch out my bra for a padded one. Better. I still don't want to do this.

I don't feel sexy at all. I feel stupid. But maybe this will get him to stop saying he doesn't want a relationship. I hold out my phone, using the mirror to check my pose. The dogs are still barking. The back door slams shut. Shit, Mom's home.

She calls for me to come help them carry in groceries. "I'm in the bathroom, just a minute," I say through the door. Knowing it's now or never, I snap the photo, send it to Ian and throw my shirt back on. I open the door. Mom is standing there. "Why did your camera sound just go off?" It doesn't sound like a question.

Her jaw is set and she appears to already know the answer.

"Umm," I stammer a lie about dropping my phone and the accidental camera clickage that resulted. I muster a weak laugh. My phone beeps and Mom snatches it from my hand.

Ian: *Damn girl, you're sexy.*

My face flushes so fast that I get dizzy. Breakfast threatens to resurface. I stare at the floor, waiting for an earful. But she doesn't yell. She starts to cry. This is worse than yelling. I would rather her punch me in the face with spikey, flaming brass knuckles covered in flesh-rotting acid.

She removes the battery and puts it and the phone into her pocket. I can't speak or else I would try to apologize. “I just don't know what to do with you, Bayleigh,” she says as she walks away and I am left feeling like the worst daughter in the world.

CHAPTER 5

Mom went to work the next morning without saying a word to me. My job every summer is to babysit my brother, make sure he doesn't get hurt and feed him a proper breakfast and lunch. Usually she gives me a lecture about how to discipline him, which neighbor kids he can and can't play with and which kids he can't see because she's having a feud with their parents, and what to make for lunch. Today – nothing. When she yells at me I don't want anything to do with her, yet oddly now that she's silent I would kill for a hug or a smile. This cold and distant thing doesn't work at all for me.

Bentley is remarkably easy to watch now that he's ten. Last year he was annoying as hell and this year he's glued to video games and doesn't bother me at all. Thank God for technology and here I am without it. Although I wasn't born with a cell phone in my hand, I truly can't remember life without one. I can't even call anyone other than Becca on our landline because I don't have anyone's number memorized.

My stomach pulls into itself. I haven't spoken to Ian since he replied to the photo message I sent him. Was he worried about me? He's probably texted me a million times.

There's a knock at the door and Bentley rushes to answer it. It's Tyler, the boy next door. His mom is currently friends with our mom so he's on the good list. They settle in front of the TV like little child zombies and play a game that's sole purpose is to shoot and kill foreign soldiers. Hardly seems appropriate, but whatever.

Tyler asks if I'm eighteen yet.

“No,” I say.

“My brother just turned eighteen and he got a job at the movies and it's so cool.” He says. He yells a profanity into his headset and then murders a dozen virtual soldiers. “He gets to see all the movies for free. You should work there, too.”

“My boyfriend works there,” I say. Ian's not really

my boyfriend but what are technicalities when it comes to conversation with a ten-year-old? Tyler shoots a few more people and says, "I bet they're friends."

I grew up living next to Tyler and his brother Marc. Marc is one of the biggest stoners in our school; of course he's friends with Ian. I get an incredible idea.

"Hey Tyler, if I give you a letter can you give it to your brother and tell him to give it to my boyfriend?"

He shrugs. "Yeah."

I rummage through my room, the kitchen and finally the study to find a notebook and a pen. In a two-page note I tell Ian everything that happened with Mom, how she took away my phone and my computer. How much I like him and how I hope he will wait for me to find a way to see him. And then I ramble on about pointless things until my hand hurts from writing. I fold it and seal it inside of an envelope hoping to deter Marc from reading it.

I write IAN on both sides of it and give it to Tyler. He tosses it by his shoes at the front door and I cringe, hoping my heartfelt words make it from my hands to Tyler's to Marc's to Ian's. It is my only hope.

Mom comes home from work with a pizza.

Bentley and I dig in, eating a lot more than usual to make up for my sub-par sandwiches we had for lunch. Something is different about Mom today. She's rigid, cold. When I had taken the pizza from her hands, I tried giving her a hug but she brushed it off. And now, one and a half slices of pizza later, she is eagerly listening to Bentley's stories and not even acknowledging me.

"Mom, are you okay?" I ask. It feels so foreign to talk to her now. Like she knows that dirty secret about me photo-texting and now we can't look at each other.

"Yes, I'm fine," she says. "But we need to talk later."

"Later? How about now?" God, the last thing I want is to fret about this all night.

She squeezes Bentley's shoulder; he's shoving pepperonis into his mouth. "I guess it's better for everyone to hear it. Bayleigh, I've been thinking about how to handle your grounding this summer."

She says it like it's a business proposition. I think she's done a damn fine job of handling my grounding – I have no connection with the outside world thanks to her. What else does she want to do, put me behind bars?

"What do you mean?" I prepare myself for whatever she's about to say. I bet it sucks.

She looks at her cuticles. "I can't control you here. You're going to spend the summer with your grandparents. And you're still grounded while you're there."

Oh my freaking God I am not prepared for this. "When?"

Mom's lips are straight. She doesn't look me in the eye when she says it. "Tomorrow."

I freak. Grandma lives in a creepy, presumably haunted house in the middle of nowhere. Even if I had a cell phone I wouldn't get reception. Why oh why is she doing this to me?

I don't say anything.

"Please don't try and fight this. I believe it's for your own good," She says. The pizza turns rancid in my stomach.

CHAPTER 6

Since I'm the only family member going and I don't have a car, I'm forced to take the bus all the way into BFE where my grandparents live. The three and a half hour drive is a nightmare without my cell phone or laptop. Mom had given me a lousy book to pass the time. Island of the Blue Dolphins...said it was her favorite book as a girl. I refuse to read it out of spite.

The bus makes a few stops and is nearly always empty, disappointing me each time by having no interesting riders. The seats smell like pee and poor people. My dreams of sitting next to a group of hot college guys definitely won't come true. I don't talk to anyone. I don't do anything but stare out of the window. It's a boring view from start to finish.

I arrive exactly on schedule and it's amazing how the bus companies do that. Grandpa waits in the parking lot of a small convenience store that doubles as a bus stop. He's driven the same black Ford F-150 truck since before I was born. It still looks brand new when I crawl inside.

"Hi, Grandpa," I say, shoving my heavy suitcase into the backseat. He nods and pulls out of the parking lot.

"Bayleigh, nice trip?" My grandfather is not a man of many words.

I nod. His lips press together in acknowledgment. The wrinkles in his face have gotten deeper and the hair that doesn't fit under his cowboy hat is grayer than I remember. We say nothing for next fifteen minutes but it's not uncomfortable silence. Grandpa doesn't speak to anyone.

We pass so many farms and ranches with massive wrought iron monogrammed gates that I start to wonder if it's mandatory to grow some kind of crop or raise livestock to live in this town. The house next to Grandpa's has a new lake in front it. An awkwardly shaped, rectangular ellipse hole in the ground that I'm only assuming is a lake. I can't see any water in it from the road. That definitely wasn't there last time I visited and neither were the dozen lumps of dirt that now separate the neighbor's house from my grandparent's.

"What kind of farm is that?" I get out of the truck and Grandpa grabs my suitcase and hauls it up the porch stairs. I follow him.

"That ain't a farm. It's a kid ruining the damn land."

I don't understand, but don't ask any more questions.

Gram knits a blanket and watches soap operas. "Who is this?" she asks, smiling when I walk in the living room. I don't know if she's joking or being serious. Gram is sweet but a little batty. Sometimes calls me by my mother's name, sometimes forgets my name altogether. She sometimes tells me the same story multiple times.

"It's Bayleigh," I say, hugging her carefully to avoid becoming a Cyclopes with one of her knitting needles.

"It's so good of you to come visit me. Old ladies never get any attention."

I suspected this. Mom didn't tell her this was my punishment, but made it seem like I wanted to come see her. Right, because no internet and no cell phone is exactly how I want to spend my entire summer.

At least the food is good. We eat dinner at exactly six. Play cards for an hour after that. Watch the eight o'clock news and then go our separate ways for bed. Only it's eight-thirty and I'm not sleepy. The crickets and the howling wolves outside aren't sleepy either. I don't hear a single car honk or loud bumping music like I would hear at home.

I keep reaching for my cell phone but it isn't there. I keep thinking of things to post as a Facebook status but there is no Facebook here. I'm only a few hours into this summer and it already feels like I've been dumped on an isolated island and left to starve to death.

I'm staying in Mom's old bedroom. It still has the same canopy twin bed and writing desk she had as a child. Her stuff is all over the place. I used to think it was fascinating, but now I hate it. All of the memories and heirlooms of my mom's just remind me of her and how rude she was to send me here. This isn't a mere punishment – this is hell.

The only cool thing about this room is that it's upstairs and has a balcony with a view of, well acres and acres of nothing, but still – it's cool. I hang out here for a long time, dragging a beanbag out so I don't have to sit on the wooden balcony. I stargaze for an eternity that is actually only five minutes. I count as many stars as I can see, and get bored after thirty-six. Then I try closing my eyes and daydreaming about Ian. Wish I could pull out my cell phone and text a status update to my Facebook. It'd say:

Bored as all hell. So bored in fact, I may just drop dead.

A voice catches me off-guard. "You should learn to take a hint." It's a male voice, coming from the neighbor's backyard.

I freeze in the beanbag chair, not wanting to move and give myself away. A shadow comes into view just to my right. I turn my head and squint in the dark to see him. He's a younger guy, definitely not a grown man but probably older than high school. He's wearing dark jeans and no shirt, holding a cell phone to his ear. I guess some phones can get reception out here. "I don't care what you feel," he says, running a hand through his short hair. It looks green from the reflection of his porch light, but it's probably brown. "You should have thought about that before you screwed that dude."

I gasp and turn away, feeling guilty for eavesdropping on such a private conversation. I'm glad he doesn't know I'm here.

"Stop calling me," he says, his voice weary. "I don't want to hear from you again, or I swear I'll break this phone in half."

I let out a deep breath. Break his phone in half? He has no idea what life is like without a phone.

CHAPTER 7

Bright and ridiculously early the next morning, I help Gram dust the obscene amount of pig knick-knacks that stretch from the living room into the kitchen and down the hall. She's been collecting pigs since the invention of time. She doesn't even own any real pigs. As we work, Gram sings oldies – not the oldies that I know, but the old oldies. I pray to stumble upon a time machine so I can go back to last week and not piss off Mom.

I can't seem to shake the habit of slapping my back jeans pocket, reaching for a cell phone that is not there. Not that I have anything of importance to tell anyone, but some random friend's text would help so much right now.

We finish the pigs and Gram makes us turkey

sandwiches and then settles into the living room to catch the beginning of her soap operas. She doesn't give me any more chores to do so I assume I'm free for the afternoon and that actually sucks more than cleaning. It is so boring here. There is no cable TV so the only channels are playing soap operas, divorce court, a show about cheating spouses and Spanish soap operas.

I decide to take a walk outside, hoping I'll trip and fall off the porch, slip into a three-month coma and wake up in time to go back to school. A police car turns into the driveway. Dust from the gravel road puffs around the four tires. Grandpa was tending the flowerbed and now walks up to the officer's car door to talk to him. I sit on the porch swing. If a cop showed up at my house I would be all sorts of excited, dying to know what the drama was about. But in this small ass hick town, everyone knows everyone and I wouldn't doubt if the cop is here just to invite Grandpa to a rip-roaring fun game of bingo in the town square. And then I hear yelling.

"You have got to get control of your town, Sherriff!" Grandpa is actually yelling, and at a police officer. God, what I would give to be able to tweet about this. I stop swinging to shush the creaky wooden porch swing.

"I understand Ed, but there's nothing I can do. The boy owns the land now."

Grandpa gazes at the neighboring piles of dirt and haphazard newly dug lake. He frowns and shakes hands with the officer. "I know Richard is turning over in his grave. He would have never wanted his house to become a motorcycle playground."

As soon as the cop is gone and the dust settles in the driveway, I run to the flowerbeds to talk to Grandpa. "What was that about?" He hands me a pair of gloves from a bucket of gardening tools.

He points to a weed. "You remember Richard from when you were a kid?"

I grab the weed and pull it from the ground. "Yeah."

"He died 'bout five years ago. Left everything to his ungrateful brat of a grandson. He never did talk to his own son after that big fight they had." I'm blown away at how much Grandpa's talking to me. I'm almost scared to ask another question in case he's used up his word quota for the day.

"So the grandson made all those dirt piles?"

He nods.

"Why?"

He shrugs, letting his face go back to a grimace. I

guess I've made him talk too much. I pull a few more weeds as penance. We work in silence until all of the weeds are gone. Finally he talks, and I've almost forgotten my question. “He rides a motorcycle on it. Every day.” He wipes sweat from his brow. “Surprised he ain't out there now.”

I smile. Grandpa's warming up to me.

After dinner, during which Grandpa didn't say a single word, I retreat to the balcony for another afternoon of stargazing and nothingness. Only it isn't yet dark, so I make do with finding shapes in the clouds.

The first cloud blob is shaped sort of rectangleish which reminds me of my cell phone. I roll my eyes. I must be completely insane if I'm creating cell phones out of clouds. My heart aches for my phone as much as it does for Ian.

A grasshopper appears out of thin air next to my shoe. I pick it up, cupping it inside my hands like I did as a child. It hops around, tickling my fingers. Catching bugs has become my new past time in this stupid small town. I sigh. I'm pathetic.

A firecracker-like roar fills the air and revs a few times like a motor. I jump and the grasshopper escapes as I jerk my head around looking for the source of the noise. Puffs of smoke sneak out of the neighbor's backyard shed. The motor revs again, in quick spurts. A man pushes a motorcycle out into the yard. He pulls back on the throttle a few times and the motor screams. Soon, the smoke stops and I can tell that it isn't really a motorcycle, at least not a Harley type motorcycle. It's a dirt bike. The recreational kind my brother wants so badly. Now that I get a better look at the guy, he's closer to my age. He's wearing these funky-looking red and black pants and a white undershirt. Muscles ripple through his arms as he grips the handlebars.

I grab a hold of the wooden rails of the balcony, pull my face up to the crack between them and watch. He can't see me, but I can see him. For the time being, my cell phone is the last thing on my mind.

CHAPTER 8

Like some kind of creepy stalker, I watch him for the next hour. He rides laps around his yard using the piles of dirt as jumps. Once he landed on the front wheel first and almost flew over the front of the handlebars. I thought I would scream in horror for a second. He put on a helmet after that and my secret presence got to remain a secret.

When the sun shuffles behind the trees enough to make it harder to see, he shuts off the bike and props it up on a metal stand. My feet tap against the railing. I want to talk to him, learn his name, get to know him. Yelling from the balcony hardly seems like the way to make a good first impression. It's almost dark so I have no reason to be casually walking around outside so I could "bump" into him. Leaning into my beanbag, I think. And then I cough. It's accidental at first, a piece of dust caught in my throat, but then it gives me an idea.

I suck in a deep breath and force myself to cough again. It sounds unconvincingly fake and worse, he doesn't notice it. He keeps working on his bike, the back tire is off now and he's holding the chain in his hand. He takes off his shirt and uses it to wipe the sweat from his forehead. Oh my god, oh my god. Ian doesn't look like that with no shirt on. I walk back into my room, pace in front of the mirrored dresser. What can I do to get his attention?

Mom's childhood bookshelf displays her collection of snow globes, each cheesier than the one before it. It would be a shame if one fell off the balcony...

"Oh my god, no!" My mouth stays open. My hand grasps my chest. I lean over the railing, seeing all of the broken pieces. Pretend to actually give a damn about them. "This sucks," I say, louder than a normal person would talk. I run my hand through my hair, try to look dejected and sneak a glance in his direction. He's watching me from the overturned plastic bucket he's using as a chair. Bingo.

I run through the house, down the stairs and out

into the yard. Dropping to my knees, I pick up the pieces of the snow globe and turn them over in my hand. The ground crunches behind me. I whip around, faking surprise.

"Hi," he says. He does a little hand wave.

"Hello." I stand up and shake his outstretched hand. "I'm Bayleigh." It's warm and kind of sweaty.

"I'm Jace. What happened?"

"I dropped it, and it rolled off." I let the pieces fall back onto the grass, frowning. "It's definitely not repairable."

"That blows," he says. "Do you collect snow globes?"

"It was my mom's. That room was hers and it still has all of her stuff in it."

He looks up at the open balcony doors, then back at me. His eyes are green. "So this is your grandparent's house?" he asks. I nod. "I don't think I've seen you around here."

"I'm just visiting for the summer," I say. "The whole summer," I add with a groan.

"The whole summer in this hick town? Welcome to my nightmare." We laugh, and he has no idea how much his presence is going to make my summer a whole lot better.

"There's really nothing to do here," I say. "What

are your plans for tonight?"

He shrugs. "I'm just going to watch HBO."

"I love HBO, but my grandparents don't have cable," I say. I've never actually watched HBO, but I bet I would like it. Especially with Jace.

He chews on his lip, deciding I guess, if he should take my bait or not. He takes it. "Want to come watch it?"

Instead of showing how excited I am, I shrug. "Sure."

His house looks just like my grandparent's house on the inside. Oldish and full of knick-knacks, including a stuffed deer head mounted on top of the fireplace. He catches me looking around the living room and probably notices the cringe on my face.

"Yeah, umm I didn't decorate the place," he says, motioning to the stuffed quail on the mantle. He opens the fridge and takes out a Coke. "You want a drink? I've got Coke, Mountain Dew, sweet tea..."

"Coke is cool, thanks." He tosses a cold can to me. I wait a second to open it so it won't explode. "So if you didn't decorate the place, who did?"

"My grandfather." He plops into the recliner and I sit on the black leather couch closest to him.

"Do you live with him?" Judging from the Grandpa/Cop talk earlier, Jace's grandfather is dead. But

I'm not about to act like I already know that. He shakes his head, looking uncomfortable when he says, "He died a few years ago, cancer. Left me the whole house and everything he owned." He opens his arms wide, gesturing to the house around us.

"I'm sorry for your loss," I say.

He shrugs. "Eh, I never really knew him that well. Him and my dad had a falling out and they never spoke, so I dunno."

"Wow, he left everything to you and you didn't even know him?"

"Well he had no one else in his life," Jace says.

"And you just live here without changing anything?" I pop open my Coke. He's drinking from his can and his eyes dart over to me while the can is still to his mouth. It's cute.

"Nah, I live in California. I just came here for the summer. Take inventory of what is now mine and all..." he trails off and I decide to drop it. Besides, I don't want to know about his dead grandfather anyway. I want to know about him. The living, breathing, super sexy guy sitting across from me.

"So you're from the West Coast and you like dirt bikes." I smile. I try to make it a coy, sexy smile but I don't know if it works or not.

"It's a little more than like, girl. It's my entire life."

He sounds way too serious to be joking, but sports can't be people's entire lives, can they?

"What do you mean?"

He flips through the channel guide on the TV. "This movie is hilarious, wanna watch?"

I nod. I'm always down for a funny movie. "So what do you mean?" I ask again. He looks at me in this weird way, like he doesn't trust me. And it's kind of insulting because I'm in his house, I should be the untrusting one here, not the tall muscley guy. The silence gets long and awkward. "Okay fine, don't tell me." I look at the TV and not at him.

He leans forward in his chair, clasping his hands together. "Sorry, I know that's rude of me but I'm not in the habit of telling people about my career right now."

"Career? Yeah you should definitely tell me," I say with a smile and a lighthearted laugh hoping it will make him tell me his deep dark secret. "You can't possibly be old enough to have a career."

He makes this what-the-hell face and spills, "I race motocross for a living. You can go pro at eighteen. It's my first year of being a pro. You know, getting paid to ride."

"Wow, so you're like really good?" I ask. He makes a half-frown and nods, the kind of thing people do when they aren't too sure of themselves. He's modest I guess. "So is it the off season?"

"Not exactly," he says. There's finality in his voice and I know the conversation is over for now.

We watch a movie in what is mostly silence and then he shows me around the house. I wonder if my grandparents are wondering where I am. It's creepy how he has left his grandfather's room completely the way it was before he died, walker in the corner and pills on the nightstand. He says he wants to contact the local church to see if anyone wants to come get the stuff. He doesn't know what to do with it.

Then he shows me his room. It looks more like a teenager's room, minus the suitcases of clothes. He's hung up posters of rock bands, and a few of swimsuit babes. There's dirty clothes all over the place and a silver Macbook on his bed. Next to that is his cell phone. I snap back to reality in a microsecond. Not reality like life, but reality like remembering that I am in this hellhole of a summer of being grounded without a cell phone or computer and there is now both right in front of me.

"Jace, I know we don't know each other very well, but do you think I could please, please borrow your phone to call my friend real fast?" I beg him.

He nods. “Sure, knock yourself out.”

I grab his phone and dial Becca's number. “Thanks so much, I'll only be a second. It's just that my phone…broke…and I haven't been able to call my best friend for days.”

He smiles and holds out his hand to shush me. “Yeah, it's cool. I'll just be in the living room when you're done.”

“Thanks,” I say again. Press send. Becca says hello more high pitched than normal, confused about the random number calling her.

”Hey, it's me.”

“Bayleigh? Where are you? Did you lose your phone again?” God her voice reminds me of home. I laugh, like a mad woman. I am so happy to hear her voice.

“No, you're never going to believe this shit. Mom took away my phone.”

“No way! That's weak.”

“It gets worse,” I say. “She sent me to my grand-parent's house for the whole damn summer.” There's silence for a minute, she's totally speechless and I don't blame her. This is almost too shitty to believe.

“Dude,” she says. “I'm sorry. I thought you were pissed about Ian and just ignoring the world.”

“Nah, I'm grounded. Wait – what do you mean

about Ian?"

There is an awful, gut-wrenching pain in her voice. "You don't know yet…"

"I don't know what?" I shout, probably loud enough for Jace to hear. "What don't I know?"

"Stacia, you know that girl from the party?" she says slowly. Very, very slowly.

"Yes, I freaking know her, now tell me!" God, I hate being titillated.

"She updated her Facebook to being in a relationship..."

"And…?" I say, my heart beating rapidly beneath my chest.

Her voice is sad. "With Ian."

"Guuhhat?" Jace's iPhone weighs a thousand pounds in my hand.

"I'm sorry, Bay, I really am." Her voice seems far away. Three seconds go by and I take a deep breath. I guess I shouldn't be surprised. Of course he wouldn't wait for me to get back. I mumble some kind of goodbye and hang up the phone, using all of my willpower not to throw it across the room.

The wooden doorframe squeaks and Jace leans against it. "Something wrong?" he asks.

I turn to face him, my jaw set tightly so I won't cry. "Nope."

CHAPTER 9

Grandma notices the extra time I spend in the bathroom the next day. The one and only bathroom has a small mirror so I chose to flat iron my hair in front of a big mirror in the den.

"Why are you wasting so much time on your hair, child?" She's shopping for clothes from a catalog designed for old women. I shrug, taking a seat next to her. There's really no need to lie to Grandma like I would to Mom since Grandma doesn't think I have an ulterior motive to everything I do. She asks if I am interested in any of the blouses on page seven. I am definitely not.

My hair is completely flat. My side bangs perfectly swoop across my forehead. But I keep sliding the flat iron over the locks, as therapy. The Ian thing is bugging me, though the Jace thing is an icing on top of the problem cake. I wish I had my phone and my computer. My ears start to burn as the flat iron gets too close to them.

"There are some brownies in the kitchen for you. I made a double batch since I know you teenagers can eat a lot."

"Grandma, there's just one of me," I say, wondering if she's noticed the five pounds I put on last year. Regardless, I unplug my flat iron, find them on the counter and start eating one.

"Eddie and I can't eat much sugar, so you make sure to eat them all before they go bad."

Eat them all? There's like two dozen of them and they are roughly the size of my palm. I stuff the rest of my brownie into my mouth, wrap another one in a paper towel and bring it back to the living room.

Carefully, I think of a way to word it so she doesn't realize who I am talking about. "Grandma, could I take some to my friend next door?"

She doesn't look up from her catalog. "Sure honey, that would be fine."

I dive into the kitchen and wrap up most of the brownies. Then I take out a few, because who am I kidding, I will definitely eat them. I had spent most of the night in bed trying to think of a good excuse to go back over to Jace's, and food is the best possible excuse. Boys can't say no to food.

Back in my room, I get dressed and assess myself in the mirror. My hair and makeup are great. My outfit is iffy, but I still can't wear shorts because my legs haven't faded from the burnt orange they turned when Becca talked me into getting a spray tan with her last week. I check out the window for Jace and am delighted to see him on his back porch working on his dirt bike. It's a little past noon, the perfect time for brownies.

It takes a lot to stop myself from skipping across the yard to his house, but I manage to walk as coolly as possible. When I am only a few feet away, he still hasn't looked up yet and I feel like he should have heard me coming by now. I clear my throat. "Hey, you."

"Morning," he says, leaning in close to the bike's motor. His eyes squint as he tightens or loosens something with a tool. I get closer and am only a foot away now and he still doesn't look up. Holding out my arms, I say, "I brought you some brownies."

Now he looks up. He pops off the Tupperware lid with dirty hands and stuffs a brownie in his mouth.

"Mmm..." The huge brownie is gone in twenty seconds flat.

"Wow, fatass, you want another one?" I ask. Being cocky is how I first got Ian's attention. He drops his tool; it looks like a T-shaped wrench. He's smiling so I know he isn't offended.

"Watch it, girl," he says. But he takes another brownie and I laugh. I sit beside him on the porch, grab a handful of screws and play with them.

"Don't lose those," he warns, eyeing me like I'm a child in a museum.

"So what are your plans for the day?" I ask. I throw in a sigh so it sounds casual and not at all like I'm hinting to hang out with him. But I am totally hinting to hang out with him so I hope he offers.

"No one ever has plans in this damn town. There's nothing you could possibly do here that doesn't involve having a plane ticket to somewhere else." He takes a screw from my hand and fastens it back onto the bike. One by one, they leave my hand and go back where they belong.

"I don't have plans either." Standing up, I dust off my hands on my jeans. "I brought a stack of DVDs from home, so I'll probably just watch movies all afternoon." I lace my fingers and stretch out my arms in front of me, and then I do the same behind my back. I take a step back, faking like I'm about to leave. He shoves his toolkit away and stands up beside me.

"What kind of movies?" A smile crawls onto his face. He wipes away the sweat from his forehead and my heart beats faster, knowing that I won.

"About a hundred of them actually," I say. His smile is contagious. I tell him about the case of DVDs I've been working on for years and how I toss out the plastic cases because there wasn't enough room for so many movies on my shelves.

"I think you should go get that shit immediately," he says. "I'll order us a pizza and we can veg all night."

I practically skip home, full of excitement and win and awesomeness. I grab my DVD case, my favorite pillow and some lip-gloss and run downstairs. Grandma is walking through the kitchen when I get there. She hasn't asked me to keep her updated about what I do, but I feel like it's probably best if I tell her anyway.

"Grandma, I'm going to go watch movies at my friend's house next door, okay?" I'm almost out of breath from taking the stairs two at a time.

She nods. "That's fine, honey." Behind me, Grandpa clears his throat. Turning on my heel, I see him standing in the doorway, a solemn look on his face. I probably look like a deer in the headlights when my eyes meet his. He doesn't say anything though, he just stares at me, waiting for me to turn around and disappoint him by hanging out with the enemy.

I force a smile, tell him bye and slip out the back door, doing exactly what he fears.

Jace answers the door with the phone to his ear. "Pepperoni cool with you?" he asks, letting me in. I nod and he finishes ordering the pizza. "We've got twenty-five minutes till they're here." He pours two sodas and hands one to me. "I also ordered cheese bread but I'm in a pretty horrible mood so I might eat it all."

We sit on opposite ends of the couch and watch a movie from my giant selection. When the pizza arrives, I'm starving but only grab one piece so as not to look like a cow. I keep waiting for him to scoot closer to me, put an arm around me, anything. This is what guys are supposed to do when alone with a girl. So far, nothing but small talk. Pointless, stupid small talk. We talk about the movie, how the lead actor just had his second illegitimate child with another mistress in real life. He tells me about California and how pretty it is. I get so sick of small talk.

I can't look at his gorgeous lips while they tell me anything else tonight. I want them on mine.

"Do you have a girlfriend back at home?" I ask, freeing myself from the shackles of small talk.

"Nah." He examines his fingernails. "Not anymore at least."

I resist the urge to ask why. It doesn't matter why – he's single and so am I. "Girlfriends are overrated anyhow," I say. He downs the last bit of his drink and crunches on an ice cube. "So you don't have a girlfriend either, eh?"

"Oh shut up." I take a second slice of pizza from the box on the coffee table. It started with eight slices and is now down to two. "So did you come here by yourself? Why didn't you bring friends or something?"

He thinks about my question for a while before he answers. "I don't have any friends I could spend a summer with…they would drive me insane after a week." He looks over at me but doesn't really see me. His eyes are troubled. "Plus I deserve to spend a summer alone."

"Why would anyone deserve isolation? That's harsh," I say. He shakes his head.

"I'm gonna need a drink if I'm going to tell you this story," he says, getting up and taking his glass into the kitchen. I follow him. He pours another coke and drops two shots of Jack Daniels in it. I slide my glass across the counter, next to his.

"Me too," I say. He glares at me. "You're too young to drink."

"So are you."

"So."

"One shot?"

He sighs. I win. He measures out one shot in a shot glass and then pours it into my drink. We go back to the living room, leaving the bottle of Jack on the counter. I take a few sips and when he's fully immersed in the movie, I excuse myself to go get a paper towel. Once in the kitchen, I guzzle half of my drink and fill the rest with Jack. I've never drank before, so this should be fun. I join him back on the couch, only this time I sit closer.

"So tell me the story," I say, rubbing shoulders with him. "Why do you deserve a summer of isolation?"

He laughs. "I lied. I'm not telling you."

I lift an eyebrow. "You're not like a murderer or anything…?"

"If I was, you wouldn't still be alive right now." His answer doesn't comfort me, but as I take another sip and feel the liquor warming my throat down to my stomach, I stop caring.

A few sips more and I'm rocking side to side in my skull. I'm pretty sure I'm not moving outwardly, but it's getting harder and harder to keep my body still. Jace is slouched in the couch, relaxed and all I want to do is get up and move around. I snuggle closer to him, resting my head on his shoulder.

Images of Ian fade into the background of my mind. "This night is exactly what I needed," I murmur between quiet parts of the film.

His hand grabs my knee and squeezes. "Me too."

CHAPTER 10

I wake up in my bed the next morning to the taste of vomit rushing up my throat. I trip out of bed tangled in my sheets but manage to find the bathroom before making a huge mess on the floor. It's all watery and tastes like sewer but eventually it's gone and I make my way back to bed. My head throbs with the pain of a thousand concussions. With the sun up, it looks to be about nine in the morning.

Covering my head with my comforter, I pass out again in hopes of waking up better. I don't. I wake up a few minutes later to throw up some more. It tastes even worse this time. I try washing out my mouth with water, but every gurgle and swish makes me feel sicker.

Grandma knocks on the bathroom door that is cracked open as I sit on the edge of the tub gripping the sides of my head.

"Are you sick?" she asks. I nod and groan. "Let me see if you have a fever." I let her press her hand to my forehead although I know it's pointless. I am definitely sick, but it's not a fever type of sick. She rests her hand on me for a minute then shakes her head. "No, you feel fine."

"I think I just ate something bad," I say. The perfect excuse. I've used it to skip school a dozen times because there's no way to prove it. She hands me some stomach medicine from the shelf behind the mirror and I gladly swallow the soothing pink liquid. She seems concerned for a moment and then she and tells me a story about when she was a teenager and broke both of her wrists falling out of a tree. I try to smile and pay attention to the story but the second she's done, I bolt back to my room and close the door, preferring to be sick in privacy.

My bed is a comfortable prison for the next several hours. I drift into sleep for a bit and then get jolted awake with the urge to puke. Grandma doesn't check on me, but I can hear her soap operas on the TV so I'm not insulted by her lack of care. Grandma doesn't leave the couch at all when her shows are on.

Somewhere between a minute and an hour later, I'm not sure because I keep falling in and out of sleep, Grandma comes to my bedside and hands me the phone.

"Hello?" I mumble.

"Bayleigh? Grandma says you're sick, what's wrong?" It's Mom. Just about the last person I want to hear from.

"Yeah, I'm okay," I say, trying to sound more cheerful than I am. "I think I ate something bad, I just keep throwing up."

"I'm sorry, I wish I was there to take care of you. Grandma isn't one for nurturing." She was right about that, and there is a sympathy in her voice that I hope is regret for grounding me.

"I'll be alright. I'm grounded, so I just have to survive, remember?" It was wrong of me to say this, but at the moment I just don't give a damn. She ruined my summer and she deserves to get a guilt trip for it.

"Well maybe this will help you remember how to follow the rules at home. Goodbye, Bayleigh." She hangs up and I'm left lying in bed, hangover, with a dial tone droning into my ear. What I wouldn't give to have my computer to Google hangovers and how long they take to recover from.

By afternoon, I'm starving. Without a cell phone or television or computer, I have no idea what time it is. Perhaps I should make a sundial on the balcony, I think. My stomach feels better but my head feels like it's stuck in a vise, every pulse of my heart causes a sharp pain in my temples.

It takes a long while for me to psych myself up enough to get out of bed and venture down to the kitchen. Normally, I would have known exactly how long because my cell phone never leaves my hand when I'm in bed. I could have been texting Becca, or even Ian since if I wasn't grounded, he wouldn't have found another girl to occupy his time.

Grandma ignores me from the couch as I fumble around the kitchen, looking into the pantry and fridge for something to eat. There's a ton of food here, but nothing looks appetizing. I stare into the fridge until I start to feel woozy from standing. A jar of grandma's homemade pickles beckons to me and I grab it, my mouth watering at the thought of pickle juice.

I sit at the table eating pickles off a fork stabbed straight into the jar. A doorbell rings and at first I think it comes from the TV, but then Grandma gets up and answers the door. From my place in the kitchen, I can see Grandma's back but not the unexpected visitor.

"Bayleigh left these at my house yesterday." It's Jace' voice.

"Who are you?" Grandma asks. It doesn't sound hostile but it isn't very friendly either.

"I'm Jace Adams, ma'am. I live next door." I smirk while chewing my pickles. He sounds so polite and proper like how Ian used to talk to my mom. Guys are so good at faking manners.

"She's sick but I'll be sure to give it to her." The door closes and I stand up from the kitchen table using my hands to push me out of my chair. I'm still woozy. Grandpa's cowboy boots stomp down the stairs. It's louder and faster than usual and stops me from leaving the kitchen.

"Why was that kid here?" he demands. Grandma says, "He was bringing Bayleigh's movies back." He follows her into the kitchen where she sets my DVDs on the table next to me. She smiles, not at all fazed about Grandpa leering over her shoulder, and returns to the couch a moment later. Grandpa stays, standing in front of me, arms crossed. I slowly put the lid on the pickle jar, tightening it longer than necessary hoping he will leave.

"Why the hell did that boy have your things?"

Grandpa's eyes lock on mine. His wrinkled face normally looks like he is frowning but right now he has on a real frown. Disappointed and angry, it makes his normal face seem jolly.

"I left it at his house when we watched a movie," I say, looking at the movie case and not at Grandpa whose grimace grows more frightening every second.

"You are not allowed to associate with him."

"He's a nice guy," I protest.

"He wrecked his grandfather's land. He's probably wrecking the house too," Grandpa's finger points at me. "And you are not to see him." His weathered finger points sternly in my face. He turns to leave and I mutter under my breath, "That's stupid." Immediately, I regret it.

Grandpa stops, turns on his heel and walks back to me. I cower in my chair. His eyes are so dark they appear to be black. "Your Grandma may be fooled, but I know why you are here. You're grounded because you can't behave for your mother. And I am not-" he pauses until I glance up at him, "-going to put up with it."

CHAPTER 11

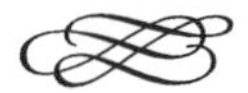

The deep growl of Jace's dirt bike fills the air. I had woken up to the sound, eaten breakfast and lunch to the sound and now as I stare at the ceiling, I fear I will be driven mad by the sound. He's really riding hard today, hell-bent on mastering a new jump he constructed with the bulldozer late last night. It is twice as long as the house and the pile of dirt that launched him in the air is at least twenty feet tall.

I roll over on my bed – Mom's bed – and trace the stitches on the antique quilt I'm lying on with my finger. Still humiliated and awkward from the talk with Grandpa last night, I had left my room as little as possible today. And there isn't a damn thing to do in this room besides break more snow globes, a last resort I am close to taking.

All I can think about is Jace. His toned chest covered in sweat, his chuckle at the funny parts in movies, everything. Even his longer than usual nerdy-shaped face and the hair that is constantly in his eyes. It is all cute to me and I miss it and want to be hanging out with him right now. I don't want to be thinking about the Ian rumors, or my friends, or wondering how many Facebook messages are unread on my computer back at home.

Jace's bike zooms over the jump again. Though I can't see it from my position on the bed, I've memorized the rhythm of motor sounds. This is so unhealthy. Teenagers are supposed to be active, not lazy. I'm more exhausted now than I've ever been at home and I haven't broken a sweat in days. I'm not much of a runner, but maybe I should go for a jog.

My Chuck Taylors substitute for running shoes and I haven't packed a sports bra so my jog will be a bit painful. But I don't care – I need to get out of the house and running is the only thing to do when you don't have a car or friends or a freaking life.

I sprint out of the house without saying bye to Grandma on the couch or Grandpa outside tending to his garden. It's a little past noon so the hot summer sun threatens to drench me in sweat by the time I reach the end of the street. I jog slowly, wanting to get as far away from the house as possible but knowing from gym class last year that I only have a mile or so until my legs give out. I've never been one for staying in shape.

Jace's dirt bike is now a distant hum among the other sounds of summer in this sad town. Two dogs compete in a bark-off to my right and to my left an old lady on a tractor mows her yard. All of these people are so old. Jace and I are probably the only teenagers for miles and I'm not even allowed to hang out with him.

When I reach the stop sign, I stop. My chest is tight as I pant for air. My calves ache and my heels probably have blisters on them. Soaked in sweat, I curse myself for not bringing a bottle of water. There's two dollars in the pocket of my shorts and a gas station is down the road to my left. How far – I don't know. I hadn't paid attention when Grandpa drove past it but I am pretty sure it is closer than it would be to jog back to the house. Plus I don't really care because my plan is to stay away from my moth-ball-scented room as long as possible.

Tired of running, I walk along the road for a while. It's a main road, with asphalt and real painted stripes unlike the gravel one-car-width thing that is my grandparent's street. And although this is a four-lane road, not one car passes me the whole time. I would never walk the streets back at home – there are so many people passing through from the bad part of town to the big city that I would be mugged or ran over before I'd even walked twenty feet.

Though I had hoped a jog would help, walking on this desolate road makes me feel even more alone. I have never been somewhere for so long without at least my cell phone to keep me company. With it, I could text my friends, check my email, play games. Without it I am truly, completely alone. I miss home. I even miss my brother.

The gas station isn't exciting. Of course, there's not a single customer in the store. A haggard old stoner watches court shows on a thirteen-inch television behind the counter. He doesn't even look at me when I walk inside. It smells like a musty old attic and I end up coughing a few times before I get to the coolers. I grab a bottle of water from the far back of the rack so it's as cold as possible, and plunk it on the counter.

"Just a second, sweetheart," he says, waiting to hear the judge's ruling. It's a divorce case, and the wife was an unfaithful homemaker who wants to keep the Porsche.

There's a magazine rack to my left and I pick up a celebrity gossip magazine, wishing I had the money to buy it. I wonder if he would even notice if I stole it. I flip through the glossy pages and then put it back on the shelf. A dirt bike magazine next to it catches my eye. I flip through this one as well and get grossed out because almost every page has a hot chick in a bikini straddling a dirt bike. But now I see why Jace wears those funny pants when he rides – it's all part of the protective gear they wear.

I flip pages until I see one without a seductive blonde and when I do, it's a page way more interesting than a pair of boobs. Jace's mug shot stares at me among a collage of other photos of him racing and holding trophies. Mesmerized, I read the title: LESSON LEARNED – HAS JACE ADAM'S JAIL TIME FINALLY HIT HOME?

"It's a dollar-fifty nine, unless you're buying the magazine too," the cashier says, now magically awakened from his TV coma.

"No, sorry," I say, closing the magazine and replacing it on the shelf. I fish out my dollar bills and lay them on the counter, then open the water bottle and gulp from it. He hands me my change and tells me to have a nice day. I have no choice but to leave the store, lost in curiosity over the article I didn't get to read.

I decide to walk the entire way home. My heels feel raw against the back of my shoes with each step I take and at one point, a bird actually craps on my toe. I guess I should be happy that the white poopy mess didn't land anywhere else on my body, but still – it's just another way Mother Nature is laughing in my face.

When I'm close enough to see my grandparent's house in the distance, I notice a red car driving eerily slow behind me. It's probably not a big deal, and the chances of someone jumping out of the car and kidnapping me are minimal, but my subconscious starts to get nervous. The car rolls to a stop. I dare to glance over at it. It's a newer model red Chevy Malibu and I can't imagine any creepy psycho murderer driving a soccer mom car like that, so I stop walking and stare at the dark tinted windows for some sign of life.

The driver's side window rolls down, and it's Jace. My fear disappears instantly, only to be replaced by anxiety that Grandpa will somehow know I am talking to the enemy.

"Need a ride?" His hand reaches out the window

and taps the side of the car door. My muscles tighten at the thought of riding with someone who was in jail, but the aching in my feet beg me to accept, so I sprint for the passenger door.

"Thanks," I say, turning the air conditioning vent toward my face and leaning in so close that my nose touches it. He wasn't in jail for very long, so it couldn't have been for something bad. I'm immersed in the smell of new car and crinkly protective paper covers the floorboards. It really doesn't make sense that Jace would drive a car as nerdy as this one. "Nice car," I say with a snort.

"It's a rental." He taps the dashboard like it's his pride and joy. "Yep, this baby was the cheapest model available, and she's mine for the whole summer."

Laughing, I say, "You're not going to pick up any girls with a ride this lame."

"I've already picked up one girl in it." My head snaps away from the vent in just enough time to see him wink at me and I get dizzy – either from the head snapping or the wink, I'm not sure.

In only thirty seconds of conversation, we arrive at my driveway. The road is much shorter when being driven by a guy who races for a living than by Grandpa who always seems to drive below the speed limit. I tell Jace to keep going and drop me off in his driveway. He does what I ask, but not without giving me a confused look.

"Your grandpa doesn't like me, huh?" We pull into his driveway and come to a stop beside his shed. I nod, not knowing how else to answer his question. Sitting in a parked car always makes for awkward conversations.

"He's never said a word to me, but he's always glaring at me and shit," he says.

"He doesn't really like anyone, actually," I say. He raises an eyebrow like he doesn't believe me. "Fine, he doesn't like you because you're messing up the yard and he thinks it's disrespectful to your dead grandfather."

"Ah." He looks at Grandpa's yard for a moment and I fear he plans on marching over there and causing a riot. But instead, he sighs and says, "Fair enough."

CHAPTER 12

With sore muscles from my stupid run earlier, I crash on the couch and thank god the local TV station is playing a marathon of a show I actually enjoy. Soap operas and court TV shows get really old after a while.

Even after a hot shower and three hours of television, I can't get Ian off my mind. I feel like an idiot because I knew we weren't officially dating. He had made that perfectly clear. But he didn't have to lead me on like that if he was just going to drop me for some skank he met at a party.

I can't believe I sent him that cell phone picture of myself. A cold chill runs down my spine. What if he sent it to other people? I don't want the guys at my school seeing that. Ugh, I am so stupid. Suddenly, getting back home for the first day of school doesn't sound so great anymore.

The marathon ends at midnight, and I finally drag myself from the couch to my room upstairs. A moving orange glow catches my eye from the window. I head to the balcony and peer out of it, finding a bonfire in Jace's backyard, Jace sitting in front of it in a lawn chair. He's staring into the fire, his eyes somewhere far away.

I don't know his story, but it sure seems a lot worse than mine. Sure, I'm stuck here with no friends and nothing to do, but my life is boring. He is a somebody where he's from. He's in magazines. And now he looks like the loneliest person on earth.

I lean against the balcony railing, watching him under the moonlight. Even the back of his head is sexy. What is wrong with me? I can't start liking someone immediately after getting over someone else. And yet, it happens.

As if he can read my mind, I watch in horror as Jace's head turns toward me, his eyes squinting to see in the dark. I press my back against the outside of the house, not knowing if he can see me in the darkness.

"You out there?" he calls out in my direction.

Embarrassment floods through me. How did he

know I was standing here? Does he think I'm spying on him? I take a step forward, leaning over the balcony railing. "Yes," I say. "I just walked out...I wasn't here long or anything."

He motions toward the fire. "Come on down. I could use the company."

I sneak out of the house, which doesn't require much work because my grandparents sleep like the rocks, and I cross the grass into Jace's yard. I sit in an empty chair next to him and he nods a hello. Classic rock music plays from an Ipad in his lap.

"This bonfire could use some marshmallows," I say after an awkward amount of silence has gone by.

He smiles, taking out his cell phone from his pocket. "I'll remember that for next time." I watch his eyebrows draw together as he reads a text on his phone and then types out a reply.

More awkward silent minutes pass, and I start to wonder why he bothered inviting me over if he didn't want to talk. All he's doing is texting. He didn't text at all when we watched a movie together. "You okay?" I ask. "You're being super quiet."

He shrugs. "I'm fine. I'm just...I don't know."

I lean forward in my chair. "You might as well let it out. It's not like you have anyone else to talk to." I glance at the phone in his hand. "Well, anyone who's physically here."

He turns toward me, studying my face. The muscles in his jaw flex. He slides the phone back in his pocket. "I'm not gonna babble on like some kind of child," he says, taking a stick and poking at the fire. "But, if you have to know, I guess you could just say I've totally ruined my life. I'm stuck. I don't know where to go from here."

"You're eighteen," I say. "Your life isn't over yet. Just like how I know my life isn't technically over, but it sure feels like it."

He drops the stick and leans back in his chair. "What's so bad about your life?" he asks in a condescending tone.

"Well for starters I'm stuck here all summer. Do I even need to go on?"

He snorts. "Please do."

I suck in a deep breath and let it out slowly. "I'm stuck here all summer without my friends, I'm grounded from everything including my phone which is killing me, and my sort of boyfriend just officially became my not-boyfriend."

He lifts an eyebrow. "Sort of boyfriend? How is that a thing? Did he ask you to be his sort of girlfriend?"

I shake my head. "Screw you. I don't want to talk about it."

His phone beeps again, but he ignores it. "How did you get grounded?"

I cross my arms and stare into the fire. "I don't want to talk about that either."

"Okay I'll go." Jace pops the knuckles on his left hand and then his right. "I just lost a two million dollar contract over a girl."

My mouth falls open. He continues. "I had just signed to ride with a factory sponsorship when I lost it all because I got thrown in jail. My agent says there's no way in hell they will give me the contract again now that I'm out. Apparently motocross is a family sport and they don't think my bad attitude fits in with the family vibe."

I picture the magazine article in the gas station. I knew he was a big deal if he's in magazines, but I had no idea he was a two million dollar big deal. "Wait," I say. "How does a girl play into this?"

"I was in jail for four months on an assault charge," he says somberly, ignoring a phone beep once again.

My heart races as I try to ask the question I'm thinking but no words come out of my mouth. Jace doesn't seem like he's a violent person...but what if he is? "Did you..." I start, unable to make myself finish the sentence. Beat up your girlfriend?

With a sigh, Jace takes out his phone again and skims through all the messages he ignored. My heart aches, wishing I had my own phone back. I have no idea how people survived before phones existed.

"He was a guy I raced with, and he pissed me off. He got what he deserved."

"Did you hurt him?"

He stares at me, unwilling to answer. "Oh my god," I say. "What'd you do to him?"

He waves his hand through the air. "He was fine. I just taught him a lesson." He throws his head back and stares at the night sky. A laugh escapes him. "At least I thought I taught him a lesson. He may have screwed my girlfriend but in the end, I'm the one who got screwed."

"I'm sorry," I say, feeling like I'm intruding on his very private emotions. I shouldn't have asked him to talk. He lifts his hands and covers his face, dragging them slowly through his hair. If I didn't know better, I'd think he was holding back tears. "She never should have done that to you."

I rack my mind for something comforting to say. He looks at me. "No, she shouldn't. But he knew what he was doing. I was his competition, and he got rid of me." He shrugs his shoulders in defeat. "Smart guy."

I kick at the small bits of firewood near my feet. "So when you got out of jail you banished yourself to Salt Gap, Texas?"

Jace nods. "I've officially owned the place ever since I turned eighteen. I never came out to see it because I was too busy. I never understood why a man I'd never met would leave me everything he owned...but maybe he knew I'd need it someday."

He grabs his Ipad off the plastic table next to him and searches for a new song to play. "I'm sick of this playlist. I think it's time for some online radio, eh?"

My heart skips a beat. "You have WiFi on that thing?"

He nods, his eyes going wide a second later. "Why are you giving me that look?" he asks.

I lean forward in my chair, clasping my hands together in front of my chest. "Do you think...maybe I could... um...?" He rolls his eyes, probably guessing what I'm going to say. "Could I check my Facebook? Please, just real fast?"

He pulls the Ipad toward his chest and gives me a condescending glare. "Do you think your mother would approve of that?"

"Come on, Jace, pleeease?" I make my best puppy

dog face. He laughs and tosses the Ipad to me. I catch it and pull up the Facebook app before he can change his mind. The pretty icon at the top of the screen shows me that I have one new message, hopefully a detailed list from Becca of everything I've missed back at home. I touch it and my heart falls to my stomach.

It's from Ian.

Hey Beautiful. I got your note at work. Your mom the world's biggest bitch, but it's probably a good thing that you aren't here...some stupid shit is going on. I'm not going to get into details because it will probably be over by the time you read this. I know you're grounded, but something tells me you'll find a way to sneak online. Give me a shout when you're back in town. I miss that cute face of yours.

MY FACE FLUSHES red and I glance up, hoping Jace isn't watching me, but he isn't even in his chair. He must have gone in the house while I read Ian's message. I start typing a reply, but then I think better of it. Guys don't want to hear girls whine and complain all the time. I'll play it cool. I mean, I'm supposed to hate him now, right? So why does his stupid message give me butterflies?

I erase my original reply and type something short and cute instead.

Having a blast in Salt Gap, Texas. LOL. See ya.

WARM BREATH TOUCHES my neck and I jump, almost throwing the Ipad in the air. "Dammit, Jace you scared me!" I swat at him with my free hand. He laughs. I've been standing here a while, but you were so damn immersed in writing to your boy toy that you didn't notice."

A lump forms in my throat. "He's not my boy toy," I murmur under my breath.

Jace falls back into his chair with a sigh. "Whatever you say, Bayleigh. You should forget that dude. You're better than him."

I narrow my eyes at him. "You should forget that girl, then." He starts to object but I cut him off with a wave of my hand. "You've been texting her all night. So, maybe you shouldn't be the one lecturing."

He holds up his hands in surrender. "You're right," he says matter of factly. "I won't text her again. It's not worth it. All we're doing is reminding each other how much we don't get along."

We share a triumphant smile, both of us happy with our new decision. "I'm glad you're here," he says, handing me an unopened can of soda. "I came here to take my mind off things but it's hard when I'm all alone."

"Glad I could be of service," I say with a wink. Oh gosh. A wink? What is wrong with me?

A chat window pops up in the middle of the screen. It isn't from Facebook—it's from a messages app under Jace's account.

The username is Loren and the avatar is of a beautiful strawberry blonde girl with sun-kissed skin. The message says, "I'll do whatever it takes to win you back."

I glance over at Jace, the beautiful boy who lives next door to me for the summer. His eyes are closed, his neck resting on the back of the chair as he faces the stars. He looks serene, happy. Not stressed out like he was earlier.

I delete the message.

CHAPTER 13

I may or may not spend the entire day peeking through my balcony window, hoping to see Jace outside, wearing those funny-looking dirt bike pants. And I may or may not jump at every single noise, every car passing by, and every grunt of disapproval my grandfather makes at the off chance that it's really the sound of Jace's dirt bike starting up.

I can't exactly call him because I don't have a phone and even if I did, I don't have his number. It's funny that he's so ridiculously close to me, yet so far away. I wonder if Grandma has a carrier pigeon I could send.

Grandma drinks a cup of coffee in the living room, a roll of yarn bobbing along the floor as she crochets. I plop down next to her and watch as her knobby fingers work the metal hook through the yarn, growing her creation more with each stitch.

"That's really cool," I say after a few minutes. Our house is filled with Grandma's throw blankets and doilies, but I've never put any thought into how they're made. She flexes her fingers, wincing from the arthritis and continues crocheting. It's a labor of love, no doubt.

"I could teach you," she says, continuing to loop and hook the yarn while she looks at me.

"I don't know, that looks really hard." Maybe something hard is what I need right now, to take my mind off the boredom.

Grandma shakes her head. "It only looks hard. I could have you making granny squares in ten minutes."

"Granny squares?" I laugh. "That sounds lame. Do you have any teenager squares you could teach me?"

Grandma playfully slaps me in the arm and then hands me a pink metal hook and a ball of multicolored yarn.

. . .

IT TOOK way longer than ten minutes, but I finally got the hang of this granny square thing. It's essentially the same few stitches over and over, and the yarn I'm using cycles between pinks, purples and blues that look pretty on the finished piece. Technically, the squares are supposed to be a few inches wide and then you make a bunch of them and stich them together to make a blanket. But I opt to just keep going around and around, making my square as big as it can be.

A few hours and several soap operas later, I have a mini lap blanket and my mind is completely off thinking about Jace.

Well, you know...mostly.

The doorbell rings, a loud ding dong that thunders throughout the whole house, making me jump. Grandma pats my leg as if to comfort me, and gets up to see who's at the door. It's probably one of their old people friends, so I keep working on my crochet. I'm embarrassed to admit that I'm loving making this blanket. It's cool to see something productive come out of my time that would otherwise be wasted.

"Oh, hello." Grandma's startled voice makes me look up. I can't see who's on the other side of the door. What if it's a robber or a scam artist or someone who preys on elderly people? I pull the yarn off my dull crochet hook, gripping it tightly in my hand as I stand, my heart racing. I'm not equipped to fight off an intruder, but neither is Grandma. She closes the door and calls for my Grandpa. She looks concerned, but she doesn't lock the door.

"Who is it?" I whisper. She waves a hand for me to sit down. Grandpa emerges from the kitchen holding a steaming cup of coffee.

"There's someone here to see you," Grandma says, nodding toward the door.

Grandpa pulls open the door with a friendly smile on his face. I can't see who's on the other side.

"Good afternoon, sir."

Grandpa's smile fades into a hard glare. I still can't see who the visitor is, but my stomach twists into knots as I recognize the voice. Jace must have a death wish.

Grandpa slips through the front door and closes it behind him, leaving him and Jace on the front porch. I notice Grandma peering at me over the top of her glasses and she walks back to the couch and sits down. I let out a casual sigh and pretend I'm not at all freaking out about why Jace is here. Whatever the reason, it can't possibly be good.

CHAPTER 14

Five decades seem to pass in the thirty minutes that follow. My crochet loops don't make sense anymore, because all I can concentrate on are the two men on the porch who are talking about things I can't hear. Grandma doesn't appear concerned, but she doesn't know what I know.

What if he found that I deleted his ex-girlfriend's Ipad message? What if he's ratting me out for using his phone and internet? As much as I like Jace, I don't exactly know him that well. He may not be on my side at all.

The door opens and Grandpa comes inside, alone. I try catching a glimpse through the open door but I don't see Jace. "What was that about?" I ask, trying to sound casual. Grandpa isn't fuming mad—or at least he doesn't look like it.

He takes a seat in his recliner across from where Grandma sits on the couch. "That boy next door sure had a lot to say," he tells her, glancing at me for a split second before returning his gaze to Grandma.

"Did he?" she asks, sounding unconcerned as she continues her crochet. The anticipation nearly kills me, but I can't exactly beg for him to talk faster. I stare at my yarn ball until the fibers get blurry.

"He came over to apologize for being a reckless heathen who disregarded Richard's property."

I lift an eyebrow and peek at him. He watches me as he continues, "Well, those weren't exactly his words, but that's the gist of it."

Grandma smiles. "That's wonderful news, honey. Maybe he won't make your blood pressure go up so much now."

Grandpa snorts and takes a sip of his coffee. "He said he never knew his grandfather and he invited me to come over and take any of Richard's belongings that might have some importance to me. I told him that was awfully kind of him, and that Richard had some fishing poles that were sentimental to me. I'm going over there this afternoon."

I can't help but smile. When I first told Jace that my grandpa didn't like him, I expected Jace to be angry about it. Instead, he came over to apologize. I can't picture Ian doing the same thing, were he in Jace's position.

"What ya smiling for, girl?" Grandpa peers at me over his cup of coffee.

I shrug. "No reason. That was just nice of Jace to do that. He never meant to piss you off in the first place."

"Ladies don't use words like that," Grandma chides me.

"Sorry," I say, trying not to laugh. She'd die if she heard the words I used that are way worse than piss. Grandpa must know what I'm thinking because he winks at me.

"That boy is fond of you," Grandpa says. I almost choke on my own spit.

"What do you mean by that?" I stammer.

He shrugs. "He asked permission to take you to the county fair tonight. Seems he probably likes you a lot if he had the guts to ask me." He leans back in his chair while I turn a deep shade of red. "But what do I know? I'm just an old man."

. . .

JACE CLIMBS out of his soccer mom rental car and holds the door open for me. I roll my eyes and slip into the passenger seat. "What's with all the formality?" I ask, poking him in the arm when he gets in the car next to me. "You don't strike me as a gentleman."

"Hey now, jerk," Jace laughs. "I may not be a gentleman, but I know better than to show my true colors when a girl's grandfather is watching me through the window."

"What!" I look toward the house, and sure enough, two fingers pull down the blinds in the front window, watching our every move. "I'm sorry about that," I say.

Jace smiles and backs out of the driveway. "If I had a daughter, I wouldn't let her go at all."

"Are you saying you're a bad influence?" I ask him playfully.

"Yep." He reaches over and squeezes my knee. Unlike Ian, Jace doesn't let his hand rise up any further than that. "I am the worst kind of influence. Especially when it comes to all the junk food we're gonna eat tonight."

THE COUNTY fair is exactly what I expected, despite having never been here before. The fairgrounds share land with the county rodeo, so the air reeks of horse poop and hay bales mixed with the scent of kettle corn and sausages on a stick.

Jace buys two tickets and we get our hands stamped by an elderly woman in a wheelchair. The stamp is shaped like the state of Texas, with a blue dot over where Salt Gap would be. We walk through a barn that's been converted into several vendor booths, selling things from handmade cowhide purses to paintings of Indian chiefs to body jewelry. For once, I don't care that I don't have any money. There's nothing worth buying here.

Jace and I walk shoulder to shoulder through the crowds of people who all seem to have their own agenda: the children ride the rides, the men drink beer and stare at the women, the women flirt and laugh and find ways to eat cotton candy seductively. I think I'm the only girl here who isn't wearing cut off jean shorts and some kind of plaid pearl snap shirt.

I glance at Jace in his dark wash jeans and black T-shirt with a fox head logo on it. "I'm surprised they let us in," I say. "We're not exactly the type of people who come here."

Jace takes my hand and pulls me around a blue

plastic trash can that's overflowing with paper food wrappers and beer cans. "Speak for yourself. I'm wearing my genuine leather chaps under these jeans."

I look at his legs. "Really?"

He laughs and leads me toward the carnival game booths. "Better watch out, your gullible is showing."

Jace buys us several rounds of carnival games, despite me telling him they're totally rigged. He throws a dozen baseballs at a triangle of stacked bottles and doesn't hit them once. I lose count of how many rings I throw at a painted red tube, but none of them go over it.

The carnie at the balloon booth calls us over. "Stop lettin' Kevin rip ya off," he shouts over the carnival music. "I'll give ya five darts for a dollar. That way you can win somethin' for yer sweetie."

"I ain't ripping nobody off!" says the carnie at the ball booth as he pockets another twenty dollar bill from Jace. Jace looks at me and gives me devilish smile. "What do you say...sweetie? Want me to win you something?"

"Only if you let me win you something," I retort, snatching a dollar from his hand.

The balloon booth is a lot easier because it's basically just a wall with balloons attached to it, and you throw darts at it. If you pop a balloon, you get a prize in the category of that color balloon. Jace wins a stuffed doll that looks a lot like SpongeBob Squarepants, but for copyright reasons, this one is called Fungi Fred.

The carnie hands the doll to Jace and then Jace presents the gift to me with an overdramatic flourish of his hand. "For you, princess," he says as he bows to me. I take the doll, knowing that it's just a stupid toy, but I can't help thinking that Ian never gave me anything. And I came close to giving him my everything.

I throw my final dart toward the balloons, and hit a yellow one. Yellow is the most abundant color, so my prize choices are from the crappy section. "What's the most embarrassing thing I can get?" I ask the carnie.

His eyes light up. "I know just the thing," he says as ducks under the booth to dig through a box. He returns with an oversized chain necklace with a pendant the size of my face, made of silver plastic. It's huge, like the kind Mr. T would wear. He turns the pendant over in his hand, flips on a battery switch and shows it to us. The word *bootylicious* blinks in several LED colors as Jace lets out a soft, "Oh my god, no."

I take the necklace and place it over his head. "You look beautiful," I say with a wicked smile. The carnie gives me a high five.

Jace leaves the tacky necklace on despite the looks we get from kids and adults alike. I don't know if he would have this much confidence if he were in his own hometown. There's something about being surrounded by strangers you'll never see again that can change your perspective of what's embarrassing.

We head to the scariest-looking carnival ride and take a spot in the long line of people ahead of us. Jace's blinking necklace lights up his face in several different colors. "This is fun. I never expected my self-inflected summer punishment would turn out this great."

"Same here. I thought I would have died of boredom by now." My hand reaches to my back pocket, then to the other one.

"What are you looking for?" Jace asks. I stare at my hand as if it were a foreign body part I only just now discovered.

"I don't know," I say, tapping my pocket again. Realization dawns on me. "Shit, I was looking for my cell phone," I laugh. "Ugh, it's such a habit, you know? I can't believe I'm not over it yet."

Jace pretends to look offended by placing a hand

on his chest. "Am I so boring that you need to find someone else to talk to while you're around me? Ouch, Bayleigh. I'm heartbroken."

We move a few places forward in line. "Maybe I'm having such a great time I felt the need to post it to Facebook or something."

He smiles. "That's better."

When it's our turn to ride the PukeMax 5000, Jace hops in the metal carriage and places his arm around the back of the seat. My stomach leaps into my throat at the realization that these carriages are way smaller up close than they looked like from the ground. I squeeze in next to him and we close the lap bar over our legs. His hand wraps around my shoulders.

"Let's aim all puke toward that direction," he says, pointing over my side of the carriage.

I've never been someone who throws up on rides, but with the way his cologne teases my senses has butterflies doing all kinds of acrobats in my stomach. I swallow as the ride cranks to life. I really, really hope the PukeMax 5000 doesn't live up to its name.

. . .

HOURS FLY by when I'm with Jace, and before I know it we've ridden every ride twice and I've eaten more fair food in one night than I have in my whole life. Jace checks the time on his watch. "I promised Ed I'd have you home by eleven," he says. "That gives us time for one more ride. What will it be?"

I look down at the empty tray of what used to be nachos in my hand. "How about something slow?"

Jace leads the way to the Ferris wheel. A sadness falls over me as we climb into the carriage. This was one of the best nights of my life, but the fair only lasts one week.

"What are you thinking about?" Jace asks, once again sliding his arm around my shoulders. Tingles flitter from the top of my head down to my toes. I wonder if he knows what his touch does to me.

"Nothing," I say out of habit as the Ferris wheel lurches forward, abruptly stopping a few seconds later to let the next set of people onboard.

"Doesn't look like nothing," he prods, nudging me with his shoulder.

I shrug. "I guess I'm just realizing that we had an awesome time tonight, but that only makes the rest of the summer sucky because after tonight, there won't be anything fun to do. At the end of the day,

I'm still grounded, I'm still stuck here and I still don't have a phone or computer."

"You can't think that way," he says. His hand plays with a strand of my hair behind my back. "Now that Ed doesn't consider me a soulless bastard, I'm sure he'll let you come over. We'll find something fun to do."

Our eyes meet, and I hope we're thinking the same thing. The Ferris wheel stops at the very top. I glance over the side of the carriage and my eyes go wide. Jace leans closer to me and whispers in my ear, "You're braver than I am."

I turn toward him, fully planning on making fun of him for being afraid of heights. But the moment my head turns, his lips catch mine in a soft, slow kiss. The carriage lurches forward and Jace slides his hands behind my head, holding me steady as we swoop down through the air. I lean into his kiss. His lips are warm compared to the cool breeze dancing across my face as the Ferris wheel makes another loop.

Chills prickle down my arms as his hand slides down my neck and wraps around me. His tongue parts my lips as he deepens the kiss, his mouth tasting like the best kind of cotton candy. A tiny sigh escapes me and I feel him smile under our kiss.

He pulls away when the ride decelerates a few minutes later, leaving my whole body flushed. I know I'm smiling like a dork but I can't help it. Our carriage comes to a stop and Jace taps my nose with his index finger. "You're cute when you're flustered."

CHAPTER 15

Jace's car is gone the next morning. I really don't want to be the kind of girl who waits around like a madwoman, wanting to know where her crush is at all moments. But when I have nothing else to do, I can't help but at least wonder where he is. After last night, I really don't think he's in LA begging for his ex-girlfriend back. At least I hope not.

I finish my gigantic granny square crochet when it's big enough to be a comfortable throw blanket. Grandma is incredibly impressed and teaches me how to add tassels around the edges. It sounds easy, but measuring and cutting a thousand strands of yarn actually takes a while. But even when I finish several hours later, Jace hasn't returned.

I spend the rest of the day in my room, completely alone. Ironically, I've never known the true meaning of alone until today. All those nights I spent lying in my bed at home, staring at my phone waiting for Ian to text me back—those nights were lonely. But I wasn't alone. I had friends like Becca who would stay up all night on the phone with me while I cried about Ian and repeated our entire conversations over again for analyzing. I had a computer that was just one click away from Facebook, where I never felt alone.

Now I have an uncomfortable twin bed with unfamiliar sheets, a shelf of snow globes and a suitcase of clothing. This is alone.

I WISH I could ground my brain from being my brain, for just one day. Just once I'd like to be a normal person with normal thoughts and no Bayleigh-boy-crazy-obsessive thoughts. I shouldn't care that two days have passed and Jace hasn't returned. So what if he kissed me that night on the Ferris wheel? So. What.

Ian ditched me all the time. I was a fool to think anything would be different this time around. Different guy maybe, but the same situation. Same soul-crushing heartbreak that leaves me feeling worthless.

At least I can make someone happy. Grandma thanks me for the third time for washing the dishes and sweeping the floor. It feels good to be appreciated, so I spend all morning finding things to do around the house. It's weird how these same chores feel like backbreaking hard work at home when Mom's yelling at me constantly to get them done, but here with Grandma, it feels rewarding to help out. It's hard to believe that my mother and Grandma are actually related. Maybe my mom was switched at birth with some mean woman's baby.

When the house is as clean as I can make it, I head back to my room and sit on the balcony in the warm summer air to work on my tan. At least, I tell myself I'm working on a tan but what I'm really doing is staring longingly into Jace's backyard, staring at piles of dirt that haven't been touched in days.

Grandma yells my name, jolting me back to reality after I had almost dozed off. I scramble to my feet, still wearing cut off jean shorts and a bra since I didn't bring a bathing suit, and run to the top of the stairs.

"Did you call me, Grandma?" I ask, jogging

halfway down the stairs. I swing on my arm around the banister and come to a dead stop when I see the living room. Grandma stands by the front door, her mouth open in horror as Jace stands next to her, his hands in his pockets and the world's biggest grin on his face.

"Bayleigh!" Grandma says.

I freeze. Jace lifts an eyebrow and peers at me with shameless delight.

"Shit," I snap, feeling the blood rush straight to my face. "Sorry, um—" I stammer, unable to take my eyes off Jace. "I'll be right back!"

"You'd better," Grandma says as she shakes her head in disapproval, but I swear I see a small grin cross her face. I spin on my heel and run back up the stairs. "Your visitor wants to take you to dinner," Grandma calls up after me. "Please dress appropriately."

Dinner? Hearing that word almost makes me forget about the unspeakable embarrassment I just endured. Jace wants to take me to dinner! And he asked Grandma! My heart does somersaults in my chest as I dive into my room and close the door behind me. I pull open my suitcase and dig through my clothing, trying to find something perfect for a dinner in Salt Gap, Texas.

I pull on a tight pair of jeans with intricate stitching on the pockets and a black tank top with silver sequin decorations along the neckline. My hair is a windswept mess from being on the balcony so I pull it into a ponytail and apply some sparkly lip gloss. This is by far the fastest I've ever gotten ready for a date.

My hand shakes when I reach for the doorknob to make another trip down the stairs. At least I'm fully clothed this time, I tell myself, but it doesn't exactly take away my nerves. At least Grandpa wasn't around to witness my near-streaking incident. I would have dropped dead from mortification.

I take a deep breath at the top of the stairs and try to look casual and unaffected by what happened even though calm is the total opposite of what's running through my mind. When I reach the bottom of the stairs, I find the living room empty. Grandma's voice echoes from the kitchen so I follow the sound and find Jace standing next to her by the refrigerator. Grandma points to a photo of me on my thirteenth birthday.

"She was in love with Justin Bieber, let me tell you," Grandma says, tapping the picture of me wearing a Bieber T-shirt and a collection of Bieber stickers decorating my arms and face. "That girl was crazy about him. Of course now she acts like she's too cool for that kind of music, but you know how kids are."

"Grandma," I groan, entering the kitchen and grabbing Jace's arm. "We don't need to tell him my life story," I say as I tug him away from the embarrassing display of my childhood.

"Oh I'm quite enjoying it," Jace says. I tell him to shut up and Grandma laughs all the way back to the living room.

Jace opens the car door for me once again, and I slide into the passenger seat. A girl could get used to this. You know, minus all the embarrassing stuff beforehand.

"So, where are we going?" I ask, leaning my head back against the headrest and noticing a sunroof for the first time.

"There are literally no good restaurants in town. And I know because I've been to every single one," Jace says, buckling his seatbelt. I smell his cologne when he pulls his car door closed. It smells so great it makes the butterflies in my stomach fly on overdrive. "So I was thinking we'd head out of town and hit up this steakhouse."

"Out of town? Like how far?" I ask, still staring at

the sunroof. "I'm not sure what my curfew is or anything."

"I've got it taken care of." Jace looks at me and then reaches up to the sunroof and pulls back the cover, revealing the evening sky. "There you go."

I smile and close my eyes as the warmth beams down on my skin. Jace inhales a breath and I roll my head to the side to look at him.

"I've had one hell of a time," he says, reaching up and brushing a fallen strand of hair out of my eyes. "But seeing your pretty face takes all of that away."

A million questions run through my mind but I don't ask any of them because I don't want to come off as obsessive or annoying. I mean, I'm definitely not complaining that the first thing Jace does when he gets home is take me to dinner, but an explanation for where he's been would be nice.

We approach a red light on the way out of town and I realize this is the only red light in town. Salt Gap is freaking tiny.

"Finally," Jace says as he comes to a stop.

"Finally what?" I ask, right before he leans over the console and presses his lips to mine. Electricity jumps through my body, and the peppermint taste of his lips have me hoping mine taste just as pleasing to him. "Glittery lip gloss," he says with a smile as he pulls away from the kiss, his lips almost as shiny as mine.

"Sorry," I mumble.

Our eyes meet for a fraction of a second before he leans in and kisses my neck, sending chills down my body as he leaves a trail of glitter from my ear to my collarbone. My toes tingle at his touch. I reach up and grab his shoulders, pulling him closer to me.

A car honks behind us. He pulls away slowly, kissing me on the lips once more before putting his hands back on the steering wheel. The light is green.

"Whoops," Jace says with a smile as he steps on the gas.

OUR WAITRESS IS PRETTY, and Jace doesn't ogle her or watch her ass as she walks away. I like that.

"So how's your knitting thing?" Jace asks, grabbing a roll from the middle of our table. He smears way too much butter on it with his butter knife.

"You mean crochet?" I ask.

He shrugs. "It's the same thing, right?"

I laugh and tear off a piece of my roll. "I crocheted a blanket, and it's pretty awesome. But knitting is so not the same thing. I'll let you slide this time, but don't let Grandma hear you talk like that."

He pretends to zip an invisible zipper across his lips. After swallowing half of his roll, he says, "So where do you normally live? You know, when you aren't banished to your grandparent's house."

"I'm from a small town near Dallas," I say as a stab of pain hits my heart when I think about home. The realization that the fun I'm having with Jace is just temporary, hurts more than I care to think about right now.

"Does it happen to be Mixon?"

I wrinkle my eyebrows. "Huh? No, I've never heard of that place."

His shoulders sag a little as he takes another bite of his roll. "Eh, I figured as much. No one lives there."

"What's Mixon?" I ask. "You're from LA, right?"

He nods and stares at the glass light fixture that hangs above our table. "Don't worry about it, I'm just…thinking out my options. So," he says, his tone changing from quiet to overly friendly, "How was your week?"

"Well, I learned how to crochet and I made myself a throw blanket. So, obviously my week was insanely action-packed and you should be sorry you missed it."

He smiles. "I missed you. I wish I could have

called or something but..." he points a finger at me, "Someone got themselves grounded."

Prickles of nervous excitement dance across my skin when he says he missed me. I open my mouth to say something in reply, but all I end up doing is smiling like some kind of freak. I run my hand through my hair, acutely aware of Jace watching my every move with a look of overconfidence. He knows he's made me feel awkward, and he's enjoying it.

The waitress brings our food, breaking the silence with her southern drawl. I'm starving, in spite of my nervousness and Jace must be hungry too because he finally takes his eyes off me and digs into his food.

"You never answered my question about Mixon," I say after a round of pointless small talk.

Jace gnaws on his lip. "Mixon is a tiny town much like this one, but it's different because Mixon is super famous for its motocross track."

"Oh. So are you going to go ride there or something?" I ask. He shakes his head but doesn't say anything else. I'm having a really hard time not asking him a million questions.

He must sense the frustration I'm trying to hold back because his face softens a bit. "I spent the last few days in Mixon. They were hosting a nationals race, and my agent met me there. He was already going to be there and it's just easier to see him at the race than to fly back to LA for a weekend, even though he assured me that either way I saw him would be pointless."

"Why's that?" I ask.

He sighs and runs a hand through his hair. "I guess my career really is over. He claims he did everything he could to get me back in, but no one will allow it. I've been all but excommunicated from professional motocross."

"Excommunicated?" I ask. "That's a thing in motocross?"

He rolls his eyes. "Come on, Bayleigh. Your gullible is showing again."

I kick him under the table. He smiles at me, and it's the kind of smile that he does and no else ever has. It's the kind of smile where his lips press together and his eyes stare straight into my soul, seeming to appreciate what he sees there. His smile fades a moment later. "So anyway, I am slowly coming to terms with the fact that my professional career is over. I don't know what to do with myself. I wanted to come home and break a bunch of shit, but I knew seeing you would make me feel better."

“Are you moving back to LA?” I ask.

“I'm not moving back there. I live there. My home is there.”

My heart cracks in half. “Oh,” I say quietly, moving my fork around on my plate. I'm not hungry anymore.

JACE ASKS if I want to hang out at his house after dinner. I agree even though it feels pointless because he'll be gone soon. I know I should make the best of the time we do have, but, in the end it's all just a big waste of emotions. I like Jace. Jace is leaving. End of story.

I rest against his shoulder on the couch while we watch TV, his hand holding mine while his thumb traces circles on my palm. His phone rings and he pulls it out of his back pocket. “It's my mom,” he says, getting up from the couch. “I'll be back in a second.”

He ducks into another room to answer her call and I go to the kitchen to grab a drink. I hear him talking about his uncle's unruly dogs and something about obedience training. The shiny surface of Jace's Ipad seems to call to me from the kitchen table. I glance around the corner into the living room but Jace is still in his room on the phone.

Quietly, I pull out a chair and sit in front of the Ipad. There's probably nothing good on Facebook, but I can't help myself. I log in and find three more messages from Ian, each one more desperate and pleading than the last. Why does he care so much about me now? He didn't care when I was there and now that I'm gone, he's suddenly mister romantic?

I type a reply to his messages. Sorry but you had your chance. I press send. It feels good to throw off Ian's emotional shackles and stick up for myself. He doesn't deserve me. The screen lights up a moment later.

Ian: Seriously Bayleigh, WTF. You can't just change your mind about me that much.

Me: I've learned that people can treat me better than you did.

Ian: Are you screwing someone else now? I see how it is.

Me:

I STARE at the blinking cursor on the screen, unable to think of a good reply. Part of me wants to say yes just to make him jealous. But the other part of me can't help but like seeing this side of Ian. He's all but begging for me back. He didn't like me this much when I left, but he likes me now. And at the end of summer, I won't be returning home to Jace, I'll be returning home to Ian.

Jace has another better life without me. Jace is just a summer fairytale.

I type out a reply. **We'll talk when I come back.** Then I log out of Facebook and look up to see Jace watching me from the couch.

"Why can't you just forget about him?" Jace asks with disappointment in his eyes.

"You don't know who I was talking to," I say a bit too defensively. I sit across from him on the loveseat and return his questioning look with a look of defiance.

"Then who were you talking to?" he asks.

I look away.

"That's what I thought," he says. "You know I was actually dating this girl before I came here, she was my real girlfriend, not a sort of girlfriend. But I know better than to keep toxic people in my life so I haven't spoken to her since that night at the bonfire. I thought you were on the same page as me, but I guess I was wrong. I guess you prefer guys who treat you like shit."

I stand up and grab my purse off the end table. "Shut up, Jace. You aren't allowed to care what I do. You're leaving. You're going back home, and you're leaving and everything we've done together will mean nothing. I pull open the front door. "So don't even act like I deserve better than Ian, because better guys don't stay around."

CHAPTER 16

The next day, my grandparents get all dressed up and leave in the afternoon to attend a fiftieth anniversary celebration for the town's police chief. They tell me not to wait up for them because they'll be late getting home. Grandma doesn't trust me behind the stove, which is probably a good idea on her part, and leaves me money for food. I order Chinese food and eat it on the front porch swing in a miserably failed attempt to stop thinking about Jace.

I really need to get a hobby.

I'm picking through my shrimp fried rice when the sound of a car engine catches my attention. I peer down the road and wait for the car to get closer, hoping it's the red Malibu that's been missing all morning from the driveway next door. As the car approaches, it slows down and my heart sinks when I notice the black paint job.

Then my heart flips over in my chest. I know this car.

My legs drop out from under me, stopping the porch swing. I sit rigid, holding my fork with my food in my lap, hoping that I won't be noticed. The car's window rolls down as the tires slow to a crawl on the gravel road. I swallow. I should run inside the house, lock the door and close the windows, but I'm paralyzed on the porch swing.

The car turns into the driveway and parks at the end of it, near the mailbox. Ian steps out. I close the lid on my Chinese takeout box and stand up on wobbly knees.

Ian throws his arms open wide. "There she is!"

I step off the porch, glancing around even though I know we're alone. Ian's wearing a tight black shirt and ripped up jeans. His hair hangs in his eyes and his smile is exactly the way I remember it.

"What are you doing here?" I ask, holding the container of food in front of me as a barrier between him.

He puts a hand to his chest as if he's hurt. "I missed you. I couldn't wait all summer to see you."

"How did you know where I am?" I ask.

He runs a hand through his hair. "Well, uh, you posted what town you were in on Facebook. In case you didn't know, Salt Gap has a population of two hundred and fourteen. Geez, Bayleigh I thought you'd be happy to see me."

"So did you just drive around until you found me? What if I hadn't been outside?"

Ian shakes his head in frustration. "Why do you have to question everything like I'm some kind of dumbass? No, I didn't drive around. I used a phone book. There's only one person with your last name in this town and that's where I drove." He lets out an obnoxious sigh. "But since you're ungrateful as shit about me driving out here then maybe I should just go home."

Tears swell up in my eyes as Ian yells at me. I didn't mean to annoy him. "I'm sorry," I say. "I'm just surprised." I glance toward Jace's empty house for a second and then back at Ian. His brows draw together and he turns around, trying to find what I was looking at before turning back to me. His arms open wide. "Can I get a hug?"

I draw in a deep breath and walk into his open arms. Images of that girl in his Facebook photos flicker across my mind and I use them as reinforcement that I should not accept him back. He wraps his arms around me and hugs me tightly, exactly how he used to. I can't believe it hurts so much. Ian was everything to me a couple weeks ago.

Maybe he still can be.

CHAPTER 17

Ian's hands have this magical tendency to grab parts of my body even though I keep shoving him off. We sit on the porch swing for an hour and I only allow Ian to go inside to use the bathroom. I told him I can't risk pissing off my grandparents by having some strange guy in their house when they get home, and for once, he's not being an asshole about it.

"You're still avoiding that question I asked you," I say with an innocent tone as I poke him in the rib cage. His arm tightens around my shoulder and he leans in closer to me.

"So many questions," he says with a roll of his eyes. "Let's just be happy we're together."

Hating Ian was a lot easier when he was still back

at home and I was stuck here. Now that he's right in front of me, with all his gorgeousness just smacking me in the face, it's really hard to remember why I hated him.

But it doesn't take much to make me remember that blonde girl. I square my shoulders, and speak quickly before I chicken out. "Becca said some girl added you as being in a relationship with her on Facebook."

He gives me a dismissive roll of his eyes. I pull his arm off me and place it back in his lap. "I'm serious. I want to know who she is and why I'm supposed to trust you again."

Headlights turn down our road, sending a shriek of panic through my chest. Grandma and Grandpa aren't supposed to be home this early—I'll have to make sure I tell them my made up plan exactly as I rehearsed: My best friend is in the hospital and our mutual friend Ian drove over here to tell me about it.

The car's lights don't slow down near our driveway though. They keep going and turn into Jace's house. My anxiety morphs into another form of panic. Only this one isn't so bad. It's dark outside and Jace can't see us on the porch since I kept the light off. His car comes to a stop and he gets out, then walks over to the passenger side to retrieve something from the front seat.

Ian's hand touches my cheek, gently pulling me back to face him. "I want you to forget about all that stuff, babe." He goes in for a kiss, but I turn slightly and he gets my cheek instead. I have no butterflies with Ian this close to me. I always had butterflies before.

"What the hell, Bayleigh?" He pulls back with a look of disgust. "I drive all the way out here and I don't even get a kiss?"

"Shh," I hiss, trying to shush him from talking so loudly. The last thing I need is for Jace to walk over here. "I'm just having a hard time accepting that I should forget about that girl. That's all."

Ian throws himself off the porch swing and punches a wooden wall post. "You need to learn to let shit go. I got over everything bad about you."

"What's bad about me?" I ask, forgetting to keep my voice quiet.

He counts off on his fingers. "Your mean as shit mother, your constant knack for getting grounded, you never put out, you are completely jealous of some bitch on Facebook," he points to this thumb but then stops mid-sentence. "Who the hell is that?"

I jump off the porch swing and spin around to

find Jace crossing the yard, coming straight toward us. His car keys jingle in his hand until he slides them in his pocket. His other hand holds a long stem pink rose with the stem wrapped in white ribbons. My stomach twists in knots. He probably heard everything.

What am I going to do?

"Bro, this has nothing to do with you," Ian calls out when Jace is only a few steps away from the porch.

He steps onto the porch. "It is my business if you're yelling at Bayleigh."

My cheeks flush and my heart feels like it's going to burst right out of my ribcage.

"Like hell it is," Ian growls. Jace takes a step forward, his eyes glaring at Ian as he approaches me. He holds out the rose to me. "For you," he says with a smile. With a shaky hand, I reach out and take the flower. Our eyes meet and he winks at me.

Ian shifts on his feet, looking like he's about to explode. "What the hell is this? You're gone two weeks and you replace me with this dipshit?"

"I'm guessing you're Ian," Jace says.

Ian glares at me. "If you know who I am then you know you need to leave now."

Jace shoves his hands in his pockets and leans

against the wall, making it clear he has no intention of leaving. "If you'd like directions back to the interstate, I'd be happy to help you out."

"I'm not going anywhere."

Jace lifts an eyebrow. "I'm afraid you are."

Ian grabs my arm and pulls me across the porch and away from Jace. "Tell him I'm not going anywhere." I look from Ian to Jace and back, knowing who I would choose if I had the liberty of making that choice. Jace.

But Jace won't be here after summer, and Ian will.

But Ian has never given me flowers. I twist my arm from Ian's grasp and swallow. "I'm sorry," I tell him. "I think you need to go."

Ian's fists clench tightly at his side. From the corner of my eye, I see Jace still leaning against the house, a small grin stretching across his lips. Ian grabs his keys from the porch swing and scales the three stairs down to the grass. "Screw both of you. Don't bother calling me when you get home, Bayleigh."

I look away, unable to meet his eyes or say anything else. Ian seems to be frustrated that I'm not fighting for him to stay. He spits on the ground. "It's my fault for dealing with some whore still in high school."

Jace flies off the porch. I watch in horror as he grabs Ian's shoulder and turns him around. Ian's eyes go wide as Jace throws his arm back, preparing to punch him. "Jace, no!" I run after him, grabbing his elbow just in time to stop him from beating the hell out of Ian.

Jace's muscles flex under my grip and I know I'm not strong enough to stop him. But he lowers his hand anyway. Ian stares, mouth open in shock. I grab Jace's lowered arm with both hands and don't let go. "Please, don't," I whisper loud enough for him to hear. Jace's cologne smells amazing as he turns back to look at me. His eyes look into mine while Ian lets out a string of profanities.

"Come on, Bayleigh," Jace says, linking his fingers into mine and pulling me back toward my grandparent's house. "He isn't worth it."

I don't look back as Ian's car starts up and peels out of the driveway, sending rocks scattering everywhere. Jace leads me into the house, up the stairs and into my room. Tears pour down my cheeks as I dive face first onto my bed, not wanting to talk to him but not wanting him to leave either. The bed sags as he sits in the middle of it. I open my eyes and turn my head to the side. Jace places the pink rose on my pillow.

"I had no idea he was going to show up like that," I say after a few moments of silence.

Jace runs his hand over my hair. "I figured as much when I heard him yelling at you."

I turn over onto my back and Jace lies down next to me, staring at the ceiling. He grabs my hand and holds it close to his chest. "You shouldn't do that," I say under my breath.

"Why?" He turns his head on the pillow to look at me. I wish he wasn't so cute.

"Because you're leaving. Because holding my hand is a pointless comfort right now. It means nothing."

"It doesn't mean nothing to me." Jace's words are calm, secure. It frustrates me how he doesn't realize the seriousness of our situation.

I pull my hand away. "You can't hold my hand, Jace. You can't kiss me and you can't bring me flowers. Because pretty soon you're leaving forever and I'll never see you again and it'll be the most pointless summer of my life."

He laughs. I punch him in the arm.

"Bayleigh, Bayleigh, Bayleigh," he says, sitting up and pulling me into a sitting position with him. He cups my face in his hands. "I have something exciting to tell you."

"Exciting for you, maybe." I know I shouldn't be bitter towards him. His good news is probably something to with his motocross career and I should be happy for him. But I'm finding it hard to be anything but sad right now.

"Exciting for both of us," he says, trailing his hands down my arms until he grabs my hands. Excitement dances across his face. "I just got back from Mixon Motocross Park."

"Okay…." I say, still failing to see the exciting part of this.

"The owner offered me a job. My own motocross school—giving lessons and stuff at his track. It pays a lot of money and it's the perfect alternative since I can't race professionally anymore."

I bite my lip. "Where did you say this track is located?"

He smiles. "About thirty minutes from your hometown."

My heart flips in my chest. "What are you saying?" I ask.

He leans forward and kisses me on the forehead. "I'm staying in Texas. I'm going to move to Mixon and work there. I'm not going back to LA."

"Are you sure?" I whisper, inhaling his scent as chills prickle my arms.

He nods. "I have nothing in LA worth going back for. Here, I have you." Just when I think my grin can't possibly get any bigger, he says, "That is, of course, if you'll be my girlfriend."

Thank you for reading Summer Unplugged.

Knowing her relationship with Jace is something special and not like all the guys before him, Bayleigh is determined to keep their love strong, despite his notorious fame in the motocross world and the dozens of girls throwing themselves at him in his new job.

Click here to read more of Jace and Bayleigh's story with Book 2, Autumn Unlocked

Or save money with the series box set!

ABOUT THE AUTHOR

Amy Sparling is the bestselling author of books for teens and the teens at heart. She lives on the coast of Texas with her family, her spoiled rotten pets, and a huge pile of books. She graduated with a degree in English and has worked at a bookstore, coffee shop, and a fashion boutique. Her fashion skills aren't the best, but luckily she turned her love of coffee and books into a writing career that means she can work in her pajamas. Her favorite things are coffee, book boyfriends, and Netflix binges.

She's always loved reading books from R. L. Stine's Fear Street series, to The Baby Sitter's Club series by Ann, Martin, and of course, Twilight. She started writing her own books in 2010 and now publishes several books a year. Amy loves getting messages from her readers and responds to every single one! Connect with her on one of the links below.